Ally

Shawn Flossy

Ally

PURP Publications

ISBN-10: 0-9975851-1-0
ISBN-13: 978-0-9975851-1-7

First printing
Printed in the United States

Shawn Flossy

Ally

Shawn Flossy

Ally

ACKNOWLEDGMENTS

Acknowledging my experiences, travels, and encounters over the last year has aided in the creation of this storyline. It's always those very small subtle moments in time that I would encounter an element of my next character. Those elements would grow into a person that can evoke empathy and attachment from even the most distant readers.

Ally

1

Blackout

When you can only find peace in sleep, you tend to
wallow in darkness and make best friends with loneliness.

I opened my eyes to a blurry vision, and realized I'm laid out on a public bathroom floor still in a club outfit from last night. I tried standing up but the room kept spinning. I crawled to the toilet and forced myself to throw up. Gagging and hurling up floods of clear liquid. Then, I black out...

I woke up in the hospital that same morning. Calm. Almost like I was happy to be there even though I hated hospitals. I suppose anything is better than the fucked up everyday moments of my life. All I wanted to do was relax for once. Not have a worry. Just as I was closing my eyes to return to my coma, my loud ass sister walked her fat ass into the room.

"Oh my God! What the hell happened to you?" she asked in the most insincere voice she could muster up.

I rolled my eyes as I pushed myself up into a seated position. "I'm fine. Thanks for asking."

"Look, I don't need your sarcasm. I had to leave work

early because the damn hospital called my job claiming something was wrong with yo ass. So what is it?"

"Man, I don't know. Think I drank too much last night or something," I responded to her question.

I honestly didn't know how to answer her. Last night was vague. All I remembered was taking Patrón shots at the bar right next to Mike's Gentleman Club. Then I woke up in the bathroom. Now I'm here. But, I definitely wasn't about to tell my nosey ass sister that. My mama should've named her judgmental instead of Jade.

"That ain't nothing new for you. You really need to grow up, I ain't got time for this shit. I'm grinding, getting to this money and you up in here taking a nap and shit. Get yo ass up so I can drop you off. Running up this hospital bill like you at the Doubletree. Fuck wrong with you?" She bitched all the way to the car.

After Jade dropped me off at my apartment complex I took a long ass nap. In my dreams, my mind kept flashing back and forth between scenes of last night. By the time I woke up I was damn near late for work. I got up, threw on my work attire, and ran to catch a cab.

When I got to the office I was expecting my rude ass boss to bitch about me not showing back up to work last night. And just as I suspected, not even two minutes in the locker room and here come this bitch.

"Ally, nice of you to join us today," she sarcastically shouted.

"I had an emergency last night," I said as I rolled my eyes.

"That's funny that your emergency conveniently happened right after you left last night with one of your clients." Her words made me think, trying to recollect the night before.

"It is convenient, isn't it?" I replied.

"If you like your job don't let it happen again. I only schedule so many girls per night. If you leave early every night who's going to entertain our customers?"

"Maybe you should get yo ugly ass up there and do it," I mumbled so low she couldn't hear me.

"Excuse me?"

"It won't happen again," I lied to get her off my back. She left the locker room.

If you didn't catch on by now, I'm a stripper. Most of these hoes in here like to refer to themselves as exotic dancers but ain't shit exotic about basic ass pussy. I'm a grade A stripper though. Bad as fuck to say the least. Most dudes like my thick thighs and my slim waist; which is fine with me because I'll capitalize every time.

I was doin my thing like I do every night. Twerking to some hip hop and getting paid. It was about one in the morning when I made my way to the VIP section. On my way past the main stage, a customer grabbed me and placed a hundred dollar bill in my hand. He was tall with wild messy curly hair and a pretty smile.

I took my time with his lap dance. Not sure why, just did. It seemed like he appreciated good careful work so that's exactly what I gave him.

I started with the basic straddle, both of my thighs firmly next to his with my ass up and my pussy pressed against his dick. Trey Songz played in the background while I gently massaged his dick with my grind. My top was still on so I seductively exposed my DD tits right in his face. I could feel his dick grow when he caught a glimpse of my nipple rings and the hard areola that lay between.

I leaned over and pressed my soft full lips up against his ear and whispered, "You can touch whatever you want."

I then flipped upside down, with my head near the ground, my ass against his chest, and my wet pussy near his face. When the song changed so did my motions, faster and more precise. I spread my legs all the way open into a split allowing all my pink insides to show. He gently played with my pearl with his rough hands. Then I changed positions. Simply by placing my hands on the ground and turning so that my ass faced up all while remaining in a split. I made my ass jump one cheek at a time then I clapped them together. He then let his hands fly grippin' every part of my thick ass.

When the song went off I flipped off him as his two song minimum had been met. I grabbed my tip bucket and picked up all the ones his homeboys threw at me. He then placed a hundred dollar bill in my garter. And just like that I had made about three hundred dollars in under ten minutes. I looked over at him, smiled then walked away to my next victim.

My shift was over at 4am. I collected my money, made my drop, and packed my shit. I started to slowly zone back into reality. Something about my job allows me to step away from the real me and transform into somebody else. I was more confident, more relaxed as a stripper. After I trade my g-string for my jeans and t-shirt, I was regular everyday Ally again. Same Ally that can't get her shit together to save her life.

I walked through the club headed to the back door. On

my way, I walked past the guy with the wild hair. I forgot how cute he was. He caught me looking at him as I tried to pretend that I wasn't staring directly at him. It definitely didn't work because he immediately got up and trailed me to the door.

"What's up?" He said to me when we got outside.

I turned around and looked at him. Goodness he was fine. Probably about six-four, light-skin, medium build with pretty soft full lips and this astonishing messy afro.

"Nothing much, just leaving," I said, masking all my attraction for him.

"Damn really, I was definitely trying to get you to come back to our table. You're amazing."

I couldn't help but smile. "Thanks. I umm… I'm off now so…" I stuttered.

"Yea, I see that. Look, I know guys probably come by the hundreds trying to get at you but you gotta give me your number or I'm just not going to be able to stop thinking about you," he confidently expressed.

I agreed with him. His fine ass was going to haunt my dreams if I didn't get a chance to experience him.

"What's your name?" I asked.

"I'm King. Like King Kong or King of Diamonds," he joked. We both laughed.

"Nice to meet you. I'm Ally," I said as I grabbed his phone out his hand and placed my number in it.

"I'm calling you today, Ally" he said as I handed him back the phone.

"I'll believe it when I see it," I sarcastically replied as I walked away.

Ally

2

Making My Rounds

Sometimes blood ain't no thicker than water.

I spent my entire Saturday morning in the dank cave I call my room. Dark curtains, no lights with the heater on full blast; slobbing on my pillow as the hours of the afternoon passed by. I decided to drag myself out the bed a little after four. After I managed to get all the crust out my eyes and brush my teeth, I checked my phone and noticed that my family can't seem to live without contacting me about some bullshit. Several texts from Jade rudely reminding me that I need to handle my hospital bill from the other night, missed calls, a voicemail from my dad asking to borrow some money, and email notifications reminding me that my bills are overdue. Then there was a text from a number I didn't recognize.

Unknown: Nice meeting you last night - Aaron.

Aaron? That must be his real name. I smiled remembering that bomb ass lap dance I gave him. Then I remembered my luck with men that I meet in the club and immediately snapped back to reality.

Me: Likewise

I live in a shabby studio apartment at the edge of the Lower East Side. I keep it a complete mess day in and day out. Most days I didn't give two fucks about my responsibilities. My luxurious lifestyle affords me the pleasure to slumber on a plush queen sized mattress that lays solo in the middle of my bedroom space with no bed frame or nightstands to accompany. In fact, my apartment is minimally furnished with no couches, chairs, or decor of any sort. There's my mattress covered in throw blankets and pillows, my outdated laptop for entertainment, and three or so trunks where I keep my clothes. For the most part, my clothes are scattered across the floor because I'm always in a rush and normally have less than five minutes to get dressed and leave the crib. This particular afternoon the sun peered through the sheets that hung on tacks covering my only window. I scrambled through my drawers looking for a sock full of money that I had made a few nights back. After a thirty minute search party, I found it laying on my nightstand exactly where I remember leaving it. I pulled out the wads of twenties, tens, and ones and counted out a couple thousand dollars. Then I got dressed in some jeans and a hoodie and set out to pay my debts. I started downstairs with the landlord. I really didn't want to stop by this bitch's office because I knew Ms. Mack was going to find a way to shit on me.

"Finally you pay me a visit," she snarled as I walked through the front door.

"Oh I'm fine this afternoon, thanks for asking," I cynically replied.

"Un huh, Ally, nice to see you drug yourself out the bed

on this fine afternoon. Do you have my two months' rent plus all your late fees?" She unenthusiastically asked.

"Of course I don't. What kind of job do you think I have where I can pay you five stacks out of pocket?"

"Don't come in here using that slang with me in that tone of voice young lady. You shouldn't have signed a lease if you can't pay rent," she bitched.

"Yea whatever. Just stop leaving those yellow notices on my damn door," I said as I threw a stack on her desk and walked out the door.

Ms. Mack knew the deal with me, I would pay her when I got the money. And she never had a problem with me paying in all cash even if it was a bag full of ones sometimes. Truth of the matter was I always had the money but either I would forget or be too lazy to drop it off. Either way, she got paid so I don't see the problem.

The brisk wind chill hit my face as I walked down the streets of downtown toward the subway. Mid fall on the East Coast meant snow was coming real soon. I headed down the stairs to the train and caught a trip to the Brooklyn to go deal with the dysfunctional assorted group I sometimes call family. I cop an empty seat near the door and mug the lady across the way that couldn't seem to not stare at me directly in my face. She finally got the picture that I was annoyed and looked away. Even though I could still see her looking from the corners of her eyes.

Aaron: Have dinner with me tonight

Me: I can't. Gotta work

Aaron: I want to see you again

17

Me: Catch me on my off day

I sent the text then put my phone back in my bag and hopped off the train at my stop. I had to make a stop by my mom's crib first. She lived two blocks from the train station. Her house was on the end of Hancock Lane which meant I had to pass by all the dope fiends on the corner. I tightened the strap and made sure my bag was zipped all the way, just in case shit got real. Luckily, it didn't. They must have just got a fresh hit because everybody was posted on the sidewalks just chilling. Cool with me.

When I got down to Mama's house of course my fat ass sister was sitting her lazy ass outside on the phone tellin the whole neighborhood's business.

"Stop talking all that shit," I said to her as I walked past to the front door.

She looked at me and rolled her eyes. Then went back to her conversation pretending like I wasn't even standing there.

"Don't you have a job" I reminded her. "Shouldn't you be there?"

"Bitch mind yo fucking business, I'm sick today."

"Hoe you ain't sick. You look just like you did yesterday. Weave still nappy and breath still stank," I laughed as I walked in the door.

"Fuck you," I heard as I slammed the door.

The house smelled like baby diapers and milk. My oldest nephew, he's four, was sitting on the living room floor playing a video game.

"Hi, Duke." I kneeled down and kissed his forehead.

"Hey, Auntie."

"Why aren't you in school?"

"Mama said we sick and we don't gotta do nothing today."

I shook my head and walked toward the kitchen. All I could think about was how my sister ain't shit. My other nephew, Cameron, is one and was sitting in his high chair in the kitchen looking like somebody just left him there to play with some apple sauce. I picked him up, cleaned him off, and changed his dirty ass diaper.

"Mama?!" I yelled. She didn't answer.

Normally she would be in the kitchen cleaning and cooking. But, today the dishes stood tall in the sink tattooed with food. Baby bottles scattered across the counter, toys randomly misplaced, and it just smelled. Carrying Cameron, I walked back into the living room and turned off the TV.

"Duke go pick up all your toys." He obeyed and started gathering his toys.

I made my way to my mama's room, passing Jade's room which was a fucking mess.

"Mama," I yelled again right before I got to her room. She was still in the bed wrapped up in covers.

"Ally, why you doing all that yelling?"

"What's wrong with you? Why you still in the bed?" I asked concerned, sitting on the edge of the bed.

"Oh, I'm just feeling lazy today." I could tell she was lying as she struggled to sit up in the bed. Something was wrong with her but she wasn't telling me. She probably wasn't telling anybody. And I know better than to fight with her.

"What's going on with my baby?" she said as she touched my face.

19

"I'm fine, Mama"

"Why you hidin behind these overgrown clothes?"

"I'm just tryna stay warm," I lied.

"Well, you can stay warm and still show that pretty face." She smiled. I didn't.

"What's been going on with you?" She was curious.

"Same stuff. Just working really," I replied.

"At that nasty lil club still?" She frowned.

"Yea at that same club," I said. Then I went into my backpack and pulled out a small stack of hundreds. "That same club that pays this mortgage," I said, handing her the money.

"Thank you, baby. Jade still thinks my retirement check from the post office is coming in but that done stopped years ago. Please don't tell her." I nodded.

"Mama, just call me when you need me. I gotta go. And please make yo lazy ass daughter clean up and take care of her kids," I said as I handed Cameron to her.

"She don't listen to me," she said as I walked out the room.

When I got to the living room, Duke was still cleaning up his stuff. I walked past him and back out to the porch, slamming the door behind me.

"You, lazy ass bitch! Sitting in Mama crib free loading. Yo kids stank, yo ass stank, and the house stank! What the fuck do you do all day?" I snapped.

"Hold on girl let me call you back..." she spoke into the phone.

"Yea call that nosey hoe back, bitch!"

"Who the fuck you think you talking to like that?"

"Nigga ain't nobody else out here but yo fat ass."

"You better watch yo mouth before I fuck you up. Remember I'm the oldest" she rolled her neck.

"I don't give a fuck about yo age. Answer my question, are you gon help Mama take care of your kids?!"

"Look, I ain't got time for all that shit. I be busy. I am the only one with a job in this bitch."

"Yea but you don't pay no bills. Mama's social security and the government checks for yo kids handle all that. So what the fuck do you really do? And where is your kids fathers? Why they ain't helping you take care of them?"

"I don't need them ugly mothafuckas for shit!"

"That's funny that you don't need them but you spread yo legs open every time they stop by! You a sad ass bitch. You and both they asses ain't shit"

I went back in the house grabbed my bag, kissed my nephew, and left. Fighting with my sister was typical but she really crossed the line when she got my mama out of her normal everyday pattern. I just left. My sister and my mama will forever be an open chapter in the book of Ally that my viewers will never understand. I stop by and visit just to make sure my mama alive and my nephews eating then I leave. I needed to make a run by my dad's barbershop anyway since he called me twice this morning. My dad is another character that baffles me. Let him tell it he's a successful black business owner but every time I see him he need "to hold something for a few days."

I walked through the streets of the eastside of Brooklyn with my bag tucked tight and my hood covering my eyelids. I grew up over here and pretty much knew everybody. But, as I got older I became more distant not really socializing with people. I grew up and became privy to the bullshit this environment produces. I lost my best friend to some fake thug niggas who didn't know shit about shooting a gun. Three months later, I moved downtown. I was seventeen. I never came back to my parents, never asked them for anything. I spent six months living on the streets then I started dancing on my eighteenth birthday. I perfected my craft and became the most sought after stripper in the city, making no less than five grand on a slow night. These same streets that ran me off taught me how to survive. I do what I have to do to make it.

All the reminiscing slowed me down a bit and by the time I got to my dad's shop it was almost seven and he was closing up shop.

"Baby girl..." He called out as I walked through the door.

"What up, Pops?" I said before I spoke to everybody that was left in the shop.

"You don't ever come see ya old man anymore," he whined.

"I be busy, Dad. My bad."

"It's all good I knew you wouldn't stay away for long," he said as he motioned me to his back office.

"So what's up, Pops? Why you need money this time?" I asked while he closed the door behind me.

"Got into a bit of trouble, gotta pay some folks off," he said and shook his head.

"You stay in trouble," I said and then, without hesitation, I dropped a stack of twenties on his desk. "That should hold you for now."

"'Preciate it, baby girl.. You was always my favorite. Speaking of, what ya sister up to?"

"Honestly, I don't even wanna talk about her. How about

22

you go over there for once and check on em?"

"You know ya mama don't want me over there."

"Naw, she don't want the sheisty shady drug dealing you over there. She ain't got no problems with the legal you."

"Well it ain't no such thing as legal me. But, I'll see if I can stop by."

"I appreciate it. Hey do me a favor though and drop me off uptown. I'm running late," I said looking up at the clock.

Pops dropped me off on the corner of Ross Avenue in uptown. I didn't tell him I was going to work. After I said bye and closed the door I started my walk down to the club and checked my texts:

Aaron: You work tonight?

Me: You know it.

When I got to the club I noticed it was already packed and it was barely nine o'clock.

"What's going on?" I asked Draya, one of the bartenders.

"The Knicks played the Nets tonight."

"Oh that's right. Cool with me. I love that NBA money," I said, rubbing my hands together.

I went downstairs to the locker room and started getting ready to get on stage in an hour. I took off my jeans, hoodie, and Timbs and revealed my sexy slim thick frame. Most of my clients go crazy over my ass to waist ratio but they love these tits too. I slipped on a black leather g-string and a matching bra exposing all my assets. I then strapped on my ten inch stilettos and added the body glitter for special effect. Then, I let my homegirl do my hair and makeup.

"Ally why don't you dress up more often? You so fucking

23

bad." Toya felt the need to express.

"You tell me this every week. I ain't into all that dressing up shit. I ain't got nowhere to go all dressed up."

"You know what you need?"

"Please don't say a man!"

"But you do need one. One of these fine paid brothers to wine and dine yo pretty ass. Show you what the high life is all about."

"Bitch if I wanna see the high life I'll just fire up a blunt and keep it pushing." We both laughed.

• • •

"And now the moment you have been waiting for introducing Ms. Make Him Rain herself... the fine and sexy, Pinkkkk Dolllaaa Bill!" The announcer shouted over the music.

"She Twerking" filled the speakers and blasted throughout the club as I made my grand entrance from the ceiling, sliding down the pole stoppin midway to tease the crowd then dropping to the ground in a split. Dudes rushed the stage with their money ready to throw it all. I signaled the DJ to slow it down a little bit for me. He switched the song to "Lollipop" by Lil Wayne and that's when I began the real show. I climbed up the pole just high enough that I could see the entire crowd. They were waiting for me to get all the way nasty. I did a few tricks just to get them to start throwing some money; I started with some balancing techniques holding myself up on the pole with just my arms the long way then, with one leg only hanging upside down. I then came down off the pole and clapped my ass to the beat as Wayne explained how he likes to get his lollipop sucked. Men grabbed at my ass placing twenties and tens in my strings. My second song "Throw it in the Bag" started to play and I started taking everything off. My thong came off, exposing my pretty pink lips; I came out of that tiny little bra and showed off my nipple piercings. I did all this while managing to stay on beat with the song. After my two songs were up I gathered all my bills in my money bucket and headed back to the locker room.

"Ms. Dolla you kill it every time," the club owner stopped me right before I got to the door.

I smiled. "I do what I can."

"You do more than that. Look get changed and head up to the VIP. The men up there are requesting you."

I was flattered. Just grabbed a quick grand off of two songs and its only more money out there to be made. I changed into my second outfit which was an all pink fishnet half top that I wore with no bra and the matching boy shorts. My signature look is a pink outfit to go with my name Pink Dolla. I stopped by the bar and grabbed a double shot of Henn on the rocks and made my way to the VIP area. When I got up there I saw nothing but dollar signs. All the guys were over six-four which is telling me this is where the athletes are partying. Before I could even make a quick walk through I spotted Aaron and his curly head over in the corner by the bar getting a little lap dance from some weak bitch. I laughed because I know he was thinking about that dance I gave him the other night.

I was stopped by a client, "Ms. Pink Dolla may I please have the pleasure," he said to me as he extended his arms to invite me in his lap.

I did a quick scan as I always do. First, check to make sure he has money and lots of it. He did have money; a whole stack of hundreds in his left hand. I then check his looks out, if he's cute then I can get into the dance. If not, that doesn't stop me I'll just do what I gotta do and get my money. Luckily for me, he was cute. Matter of fact he was fine as fuck. Chocolate complexion, athletic build, nice smile; just my type.

"You may but I have to disclose that I am Ms. Pink Dolla Bill and I am a certified dick pleaser. You have been warned," I said as I sat in his lap.

He grabbed my thighs instantly and put his head on my shoulder.

"Ms. Dolla, I been looking for you," he said as he ran his fingers across my body. Grabbing everything he thought was soft.

"Glad you finally found me. Took you long enough," I played with him.

"Do something nasty for me," he begged.

I stood up and turned around with my ass facing his face. He spread his legs making sure to give me plenty of space. I started clapping my ass, one cheek at a time. Then both together making sure he could see my pink insides every time I clapped. Then I flipped up into a handstand and placed my legs on his shoulders forcing his lips to kiss my pussy. He kissed her. Matter of fact he sucked every ounce of juices out my pussy while I clapped my ass against his face. He almost made me cum but I flipped off right before. I took a moment to gather myself then straddled his lap and pulled out my tits. My nipple rings enticed him to play with them with his tongue. He loved my tits so much he grabbed my ass and wouldn't allow me to move while he buried his face. Then, the song changed and his two songs were up.

"Ms. Dolla, I love you," he said as he took the rubber band off his stacks and handed me half.

"I love you, too," I said as I walked away. But what I really meant was I love your money.

I'm counting my money, placing it into my money bag when I run right into Aaron. I knew this would happen, I was just waiting for it. I looked up at him and he had this smirk on his face. I ran my hands through his hair one time and he grabbed my waist and made me sit in his lap.

"So this is how I have to find you? At work huh?" he asked.

"I'm a busy girl," I played with him.

He helped me put my shirt back on, which had NEVER happened to me before. Even though it didn't matter because my entire outfit was fishnet that you could see through.

"So do you want a dance?" I asked him while I played in his hair.

"No. I want a date."

"Aaron…" I started to hesitate.

"We can go to lunch, since you work nights," he interjected.

"But…"

"I'll pick you up and you don't have to pay for anything. And I won't take no for an answer," he demanded.

He helped me stand up then got up right after me. "I'll see you tomorrow. Be safe tonight," he said right before he walked downstairs to the front door and left. He really came to the club just to set up a date with me. I thought about him for the rest of the night as I danced and impressed man after man. Each one of them telling me how much they love me and how I'm the greatest. And the only thing I could think about was Aaron.

That morning before I clocked out I change back into my jeans and hoodie. I headed toward the door with my bag and I checked my phone.

Aaron: Noon, meet me at Central Ave.

I wanted to reply back and say no I was going to be too tired but instead I said:

Me: You better not be late.

3

Ten Grand

It's rare you find a person that keeps every promise;
those you keep.

That next day I woke up feeling like shit. I drank way too much Cîroc and I was paying for it this morning. I had to get up early so that I could get ready to meet Aaron at noon. It's strange that I'm actually giving somebody the time of day to take me out. If it was anybody else I would have found some reasonable excuse not to see them, especially this early.

The sun peered through my the sheets tacked over my window, attempting to fill the room with its rays as I moved sluggishly through my studio apartment. The floor was cool from the chilly night and my bare feet were resisting with every step. I stood at the mirror in my bathroom examining my appearance; trying to decipher what look I wanted to accomplish for the day. I surely couldn't wear my usual oversized hoodie and jeans. And I definitely wasn't defaulting to my nightlife work look. At that point I realized I didn't own clothes or even had a clue how to get cute enough for my date. My idea of a cute outfit is having a sweatshirt that exactly matched a pair of sweatpants. Ironically, I don't even have that combination to choose from. I needed help and I need it fast so, I texted Toya:

Me: I have a date in two hours with nothing to wear.

Toya promptly received my cry for help and called me to get my address so she could come to my rescue. Toya and I are pretty cool at work but this was the first time I actually reached out to her for some personal shit. Before today the most personal conversation we've had was a detailed discussion on whether or not pussy poppin on a handstand was worth more than a hundred dollar tip. She said a Ben Franklin was enough, I disagreed. I ain't pulling out the pussy pop until the real ballers show up. But that's just me.

When she arrived, she came with a duffle bag full of stuff. Literally. A big ass bag full of all kinds of shit that I was unfamiliar with. Brushes and hair oils. The bitch clearly thought I was tore up because she packed her entire bathroom and brought it to my crib.

"Damn, all the money you make and you live in the middle of the hood like a savage," she whined as she walked through the door.

"I don't see the problem," I sarcastically replied. My apartment was savage as fuck. I could afford a better place to live if I wasn't paying for a home mortgage and stocking the fridge at my mama's house just to make sure my nephews ate.

"So why didn't you tell me you had a date last night? We could have gotten you right then," Toya asked.

"I didn't realize I didn't have clothes until thirty minutes ago."

"Ally, I've told you a thousand times to upgrade your

wardrobe. You are so lucky I fuck with yo sexy ass. Come into this bathroom and let me get you right," she said as she motioned me to follow her.

"Look don't do too much. I'm not tryna look all extra. Something cute and simple will suffice," I demanded.

"Baby, you are in good hands. Ms. Toya is a fab fashion stylist of New York. Google me, boo," she said moving all her fingers showing off her long ass stiletto nails.

"Tone down the cockiness."

"Don't even know how to do that. Sorry," she said with this goofy smirk on her face.

I allowed Toya to work her magic, as she would call it. She blew out and straightened my hair and clipped my ends. Then, she dressed me in all black leggings with leather front panels, a cropped long sleeve black top and a jacket to match the pants. She finished by touching my face with MAC makeup, modest eye shadow, nude lip line, and thick mascara. I was cute, sleek, sexy and feeling myself.

• • •

It's brisk outside. Naw fuck that. It's cold as fuck out. This cute ass outfit Toya dressed me in was cute and perfect for a date but was shitty as hell to wear just standing outside waiting. I checked my phone every five minutes to see if Aaron had called or texted, hell even sent me a tweet. Nothing.

Thirty minutes past twelve and I had been pacing within the same four cement squares at the corner that I was told to be at. Fed up I turned around, bundled my coat tight, and walked back toward the subway station. I could say I'm disappointed or maybe even furious but I'm not. I have been let down by enough people in my life to know that there will be more times to come and I can just add Aaron to the mile long list. My freshly straightened hair blew in the wind and my eyes watered with every step from the wind. Luckily, I was wearing waterproof mascara so my face didn't run.

After a block my skin started to adjust to the wind and I became comfortable in my travel. I never owned my own car so I'm all too familiar with foot travel. I always wanted a truck or a big body SUV. Not because I have people or things to transport but because I like sitting up high looking down on other people while I weave through traffic. When I turned eighteen, I walked into the DMV office randomly and requested information on how to get a driver's license. After the rude bitch at the front desk told me I needed to either have a learner's permit or pass a written test in order to even take my physical driving exam I dropped the idea of having a driver's license. I never went to Driver's Ed nor did either of my parents have enough time to teach me how to drive before I took off and departed from their half ass caregiving.

So here I am, twenty-two and no driver's license. But that never stopped me from driving. If and when I could get someone to let me borrow their vehicle I whip that shit perfectly without flaw. I learned to drive by teaching myself after I committed grand theft auto and took a car from one of those bullshit ass used car lots in the Bronx. It was only a few years back but it was dead in the middle of winter and I was still homeless at the time. I needed something warm to hibernate in at least for a few weeks until I could save some money to squat at a hotel that wasn't in a drug infested area. I slept in that car for eight days with it parked ducked off behind an old trailer park. On the ninth day, I took the used Honda Accord to my boy Hector back in my hood and he chopped it up and threw me a couple stacks. I used that money to pay the first and last month's rent on my first apartment. That was the first time in almost three years that I actually had a place I could call home. I cried that night; sitting on the hardwood floor of my new loft.

I was literally a few feet away from the subway station when an all-black Audi coupe sitting on black 20s drove past. That car was clean as fuck. Brand new car, didn't even have the official license plate on yet just the card stock version from the dealer. The tint was so dark I wasn't even sure if a human was driving it. I paused just for a quick second to awe and then I turned back around.

"Ally," a voice from behind me shouted. I turned around and squinted. It was Aaron. Hanging his head out the Audi holding up traffic in the middle of downtown.

"Get in the car!" He commanded then he pulled his head back in and rolled the window up.

I was a little salty that he had me waiting for forever but I wasn't no dumb ass. It was thirty degrees outside. The least I could do was use his ass for a ride.

I hopped in the coupe and shut the door. The all black leather interior caught my attention and my whole mood changed once my entire body had the chance to embrace the centralized heat.

I looked over at Aaron who was already maneuvering his way through traffic.

"I know I'm late." That was all he had to offer for an explanation. "I'll make it up to you I promise." He was smooth. It was impossible to be mad at him.

"You know I could have been doing more important things," I snapped.

"Like what? Practicing how to make yo ass clap while sliding down a pole?" He laughed at his own joke. His smile was gorgeous. Pretty white ass teeth. I didn't laugh. I only smiled because his smile made me smile.

"I bet you thought that was funny. Huh?" I snarled.

He looked over at me. "You're cute when you try to pretend to be mad." He smiled. Then touched my hair.

"You look nice. I like it when your hair is wavy but its looks good straight too." He noticed. "I'm surprised nobody tried to pick you up while you waited on me."

"I wish somebody would. I do not play that shit." He shook his head ignoring my comment.

"So, where are we going?" I was curious.

"Manhattan."

"For what? Restaurants? Because there are plenty of places to eat around here."

"One, I got some business to take care of on the way. Two, I'm not taking you to one of these lame places some other nigga already took you to. You ridin with King today. I'ma put you on new things. Shit you never been on before or even heard of. Just relax, love."

"Why do they call you King?"

"That's my street name. You can call me Aaron. Whatever you like is fine with me."

"But why do they call you King?"

"I mean it's really a long story. I run shit basically," he vaguely answered.

I sat quietly in the passenger seat and enjoyed the ride. Before today I had never been in an Audi. Actually I never been in a car that cost more than thirty racks. I wasn't even sure how much the car cost but I knew it was expensive

34

because everything was either leather material or real wood grain panels. There were red accents throughout the car to add more character, full audio system, navigation, and TV screens on the back of the front seats. From the outside it looks like Aaron just bought the car but on the inside you can tell he has had it for a while. That made me wonder why it still has paper tags for license plates.

• • •

I fell asleep after about twenty minutes. I hadn't even realized I was tired. The car ride put me to sleep quickly. When I opened my eyes I was in the car alone. The car was parked behind a warehouse and Aaron was nowhere in sight. I looked around to see what was going on. But there was nothing. There weren't any people walking around, no cars driving down the alleyway. There were rows and rows of white warehouses and all the garage doors on them were shut. Shit was kind of creepy. I felt like the only person in the world sitting there alone.

Then the garage door right in front of where the car was parked opened up and Aaron walked out with a big ass bald, dark skinned body building Debo looking mothafucka. They stood in front of the car talking for a few minutes, then Aaron picked up a duffle bag off the ground and walked around to the trunk then placed the bag inside. Debo closed the garage door behind him and Aaron closed the trunk. Then he got back into the car. I pretended I was still sleeping.

He sped off and back toward the city and I casually pretended to wake up. I stretched and yawned like I hadn't already completed this process fifteen minutes ago.

"I hope you didn't drool on my seats girl," he joked.

"Whatever." I had no come back. "Where are we now?" I asked.

"A few blocks from where I'm taking you."

"I'm really starting to think you didn't make plans and you are just driving around trying to think of something for us to do."

"Damn. So basically you think I'm slow as hell?" I laughed at his reaction. "You think it takes me forty-five minutes and a fourth of a tank of gas just to figure out what to do with a female?"

Aaron was goofy. I liked that about him. He played and joked around, even in situations where most people would answer completely seriously he found ways to insert his personality. That made him more attractive. His curly brown hair was cute and his long eyelashes made him nearly irresistible. But his personality made him likable. Like I could call him on nights that I felt alone and I would know he would make it better.

He pulled up to a tall building and parked in front of the valet. The valet opened the door for me and helped me get out while Aaron grabbed his bag from the backseat. He walked over to the valet handed him his keys and then whispered something in his ear. I couldn't make out what he was saying. The valet nodded in agreement then Aaron tipped him and walked over to me.

He put his hand around my waist and told me to follow him. We walked through the large automated doors and into the fancy lobby. There was a big ass fountain in the center and then off to the right was the front desk.

"Did you bring me to a hotel?" I was starting to get mad.

"Not exactly. This is a luxury extended spa." I felt

relieved.

"Oh…" I responded.

"But they have hotel rooms too," he laughed. I scowled.

He checked us in while I roamed around the lobby. I'd never actually been any place fancy or upscale. I spent most of my time in the strip club or roaming the streets.

"Come on," Aaron demanded.

"Where we going?".

"I'ma show you where everything is and then I'll let you do you until dinner. Then it's my time."

"I can't stay here with you all night."

"Yea you can."

"I have to be at work by midnight," I told him.

"So? I'll pay you whatever you normally make a night."

"I make five grand a night," I said, folding my arms.

"I'll give you ten grand. In cash," he said as he walked past me prompting me to follow him.

He showed me the massage rooms, the mud bath stations, the heated pool and spa tub, the manicure and pedicure salon, and the sauna.

"Here's a key to our room. You have access to anything you want to do in here. If anybody gives you a problem tell them you know me. I'll be in the business room. I got some shit to handle. Meet me in the dining hall at nine for dinner." He let my hand go and went about his business.

I didn't know how to feel about him. He took me out the hood and dropped me off in a spa with unlimited access to anything I wanted. And I hadn't done anything for him other than give him an everyday lap dance that I would give any customer holding a hundred dollar bill. I didn't know anything about this man other than he was fine as fuck, rich as hell, and he drove an Audi. I do not even know his last name, his age, or what he did for a living.

I enjoyed every luxury the spa offered within the five hour time limit I was given. I had a fresh mani and pedi, smooth exfoliated skin from the mud bath, relaxed muscles due to the hour long full body massage, and now I was just chilling in the spa tub sipping on my fifth glass of wine without a care in the world.

A few minutes after nine I met Aaron at our reserved table in the dining hall of the spa. I still had on my robe because I didn't bring any additional clothes but I didn't stand out because everyone was wearing their robes for the most part.

"You look relaxed. Happy." Aaron smiled. I smiled back.

"This place is amazing. Like can I live here?" I exclaimed.

"You can't live here but you can live like this. If that's what you want," he calmly explained.

"Why do you have so much money?"

"I don't. I have just enough to do all the shit I want to do plus more."

"But how?"

"I have a job. Like you."

"But you not on a stage every night shaking your ass and tits for twenties," I snapped.

He laughed. "True."

"So what do you do?" I required him to answer.

"I run my business. My clients pay me." Then he put his hand against my face. "I didn't think it was going to be a problem, taking you out and showing you a good time," he said as the waiter brought out our waters and appetizer.

"It's not. I really appreciate it."

"Good. I'm glad. You know when I saw you that first night, I saw you when you first came into work, way before you had a chance to change. You looked stressed or pissed off about something. I'm not going to lie. I thought you were cute but I wasn't expecting you to come out with the body you have. Caught me off guard. You intrigued me. Then later that night when I asked for your number and you finally looked at me in my eyes, I finally saw you for the first time. You showed me something I didn't see before. I could see more about you. Or I could see more about what you didn't want me to know."

I was shocked as I listened to him describe his thoughts.

"What is it about me that you like?" I was curious.

"I don't know yet. I can just tell that there is more to your story, more to you and you don't want me to see it. That makes me want to get to know you."

"That's exactly how you leave me feeling. Like who are you? Where did you come from? Why don't you ever answer my questions directly?" I admitted.

He again ignored my questions. "I also like you because you're gorgeous as fuck and I really think you should be walking down a runway instead of sliding down a pole."

That was one of the nicest things I'd heard a person say to me in a while. I didn't even know how to respond. His words reminded me of the kind of compliments my mom would give me when I was little. Way before my soul changed, back when I was happy. She always said my smile was the kind of smile that could make anyone smile. I don't really smile much now.

We ate. We talked. Aaron made me laugh all night long

telling me stories about his homeboys and their wild ass behaviors. He didn't tell me much about himself. He told me to save some of my questions for our second date. The fact that he wanted a second date was new to me. Usually all the dudes that I let get even slightly close to me I turned off with my standoffish attitude. And then you have those type niggas that just pretended to like me just to fuck but that shit don't happen to me much anymore.

That night we watched old movies while we curled up in the soft plush king sized bed in our suite enjoying each other's company. Aaron gave me an option to either sleep at the hotel or go back home but either way he had to leave. He said he had some early morning business he would have to tend to. I told him to take me back to my side of town. It was around two in the morning when we checked out and drove back. After our embrace and goodbyes, I got out the car, closed the door, and sunk back into reality. The cold streets of New York, my drab unfurnished apartment, and my lonely mattress lying on the floor.

4

Pawn Shop

When life gives you lemons, you get rid of the lemons and find a legitimate move. The fuck you suppose to do with lemons?

I had to be having top three worst days of my life. Just last week I had the most amazing experience with Aaron and a whole seven days later, I'd yet to hear from him. I would give him a call but I dropped my cell phone on the train tracks two days ago in the subway station. But before even losing my phone I sent six delivered text messages that did not trigger one response from him. And if that didn't seem like it was enough to make a mothafucka scream, I walked into work today and my manager politely handed me a insubordination notice stating that I'll be suspended for the next two weeks because I missed work without calling the day I went out with Aaron. Which came right on schedule promptly after my second eviction notice was attached to my door and my mom's mortgage overdue statement came to my email. Perfect.

One thing I could always count on is misfortune. Today,

this week, hell my entire life, is no different. I sat at the corner of 5th Street and Penn Avenue at this little local coffee shop. I don't drink coffee, I just come here because of the location. Around seven every evening during the fall, the sun slowly lowers itself setting behind the Microsoft store. The rays bounce off the Target billboard at just the right angle creating an optical illusion that there is a rainbow sitting directly in the middle of traffic. It lasts for all of three and half minutes but for me it was art. Three and a half minutes of pure artwork created by a superior being. I sat at the corner for almost three hours before I realized that sitting here wasn't going to solve any of my problems. I had less than a week to get enough money to keep my mama, sister, and two nephews from getting kicked out their crib. And paired with the New York high cost of living I had even less time than that to make sure I wasn't homeless.

I walked down 5th until it turned into 6th and walked down 6th until I ran into an alley. It was a small alleyway that I had been to once before. On the other side of the alley is 7th Street which is known for high traffic and lots of interaction. The alley behind 7th Street was uncommon for the everyday bystander. Most people never noticed the alleyway or even if they do notice they don't care much. It's just another alleyway amongst all the others. I walked past the alley entrance and around to 7th where all the storefronts are. I was looking for Hector. Remember, Hector is my chop shop plug but without my cell I had no way of contacting him. So, instead, I walked around the same area I remember dropping off that Honda a few years back. I knew for a fact I didn't look lost or appear to be searching for something. I'm pretty good about hiding my emotions. When I walked past this pawn shop I looked up to read the name on the sign. New Money Pawn. Then, I look down at the door and noticed this guy standing in front of it. Six-two, dark skin, low cut. He was just standing there staring at me but after he got a good look he just casually moved his attention elsewhere. I wasn't sure if he was even looking at me originally because he didn't flinch or even turn his head quickly like most people do when someone notices you noticing them. It's like he took in all he needed from me visually then changed his focus. I kept walking down the street, slowly this time. As if I was hesitant to continue. Something, some kind of energy, was holding me back. I stopped then turned around and see that the guy was looking at me again, dead in my face.

"What's good?" I yelled down the street.

He shrugged his shoulders like he had no clue as to what I was talking about. Like he was lost and I was buggin.

"You're staring at me." I snapped as I walked back toward him.

"I'm looking at you. There's a difference," he said while chewing his gum. His hand gestures were giving me that nonchalant vibe.

"Well... why are you looking at me?"

"Shit I don't know. Maybe because you were just standing directly in front of me. What you want me to do act like you not here?"

He had a point. I dropped my attitude and remembered I was on a mission.

"Anyway, I'm looking for Hector. Do you know him?"

He glanced me over once raising his eyebrow before he answered my question. "Hector don't work here no more."

"Oh so this use to be the chop shop," I asked without

even thinking.

"Who the fuck are you? The Feds or something shorty?" He got real defensive, like he had something to protect.

"Hell naw. Furthest thing from it. I was just looking for Hector but I appreciate you," I said then I turned around.

"Hector don't work here no more but the business still operating," he said with my back facing him.

I turned around.

"Nino." He introduced himself.

"I'm Ally." Nino is one of those charming on accident type niggas. Full time street nigga but he was educated and understood the concept of effective communication.

After I told Nino my situation and gained his trust he wanted to know more about why I was looking for Hector. I explained to him our relationship and gave him details of what I was capable of. He seemed interested and after I further probed he finally opened up and broke down the entire operation.

"So look this how all this shit work. The pawn shop is open seven days out the week. We create some revenue through your everyday pawned items: cell phones, jewelry, game systems, and other shit like it. But, our real money "pawn" items come in through the alley. In the back of the store we have a garage. The garage is connected to the auto shop next door. Our customers drive in their merchandise through the garage, stop by the front desk to receive their cut, then walk out through the front door like every other customer."

"What happens to the cars?" I asked

"It's not always cars that come through sometimes there's motorcycles, SUVs, dirt bikes, whatever. Our mechanics in the back take the vehicle apart. Everything comes off, the windows, mirrors even all the small fixtures. All the parts are categorized by type of part and at the end of each shift the parts are shipped off."

"Shipped where?"

"Depends on the category. If we get brand new cars we sell those parts back directly to the manufacturer. Other categories we get off through warehouses or junk yards. Either way, everything that comes into the garage goes out the garage in less than three hours."

"And if you can't sell it?"

"We dump it. No evidence is left in the garage, ever. Every day when I close the store down I check to make sure the garage is completely empty and fully wiped down. No prints, no evidence, no nothing," he finished explaining.

"I want in," I expressed. I knew I could do this shit easy, I'd been hot wiring and jacking care since I was fifteen.

He laughed. "Naw, shorty you might not be ready for prime time yet. You can work in the pawn shop though, like a cashier or some shit."

"And make like eight dollars an hour? Hell naw, you got me fucked up. I'm tryna see some real cash."

"Only mothafuckas that make big bucks in this bitch is me and the runners that bring back luxury cars. You know shit like Cadillacs, Benz, Maseratis, Bentleys; shit like that. And stealing those kind of cars take skills."

"If I brought you a Benz how much do I get cut?"

"That's a easy three stacks. Maybe more depending on the model," he answered.

I was plotting. I had the opportunity to make some nice cash over the next two weeks while I wait for my suspension to be up.

"I want in." I repeated to Nino.

He looked me over again just like he did when we first met. "Man look, I'll put you on payroll if you can bring me back a luxury car by the end of the week. But if you get caught up don't mention me or my shop."

I gave him a mean as stare. How the fuck this nigga gone try to check me on my street cred? But at the end of the day I felt where he was coming from. He had a lot more to lose in this situation than I did.

"I ain't no snitch."

"I can tell. I just wanted to make sure we were clear. No fuck shit." We shook hands and I took off back down 7th Street toward the subway. It was getting late.

I got off at my stop and walked the four blocks to my apartment building. I plotted on how I was going to catch my first pawn item the entire way home. I thought about all the high roller spots where all the rich bougie folks stay. Then I also thought about how the Feds be camped out protecting the fuck out of their shit too. There's a couple places I could catch slipping on the south side but, they normally don't keep heavy hitter merchandise. They just have your everyday chargers or impalas. Nothing too expensive. Then I thought about that area where Aaron took me that had all those garages. I remember when he walked out the garage carrying that bag there was a bunch of foreign shit that I didn't recognize. They had to be worth some cash. There were hundreds of garages lined up right next to each other stretching a few miles long. I just had to figure out how to get into one of them, get the car started, and get the car back.

That next morning I got up early. And not my normal

damn near noon early, I mean real life early. Before the sun woke up early. I threw on some black sweats and a grey long sleeve hoodie, grabbed my bag and headed for the train. I had a long ass ride to Manhattan and I wanted to get it done early. On the train I pulled out a notebook that I had been scribbling in all night. I used my laptop to pinpoint the exact location of the garage center. It wasn't easy. Apparently there are six garage centers in the same area that all look alike. Thankfully my memory and Google maps worked well together. I had the exact address of the one-hundred and twenty garage lot and a map that I drew. According to the world wide web the first forty garages are one-hundred and sixty feet tall. Tall enough to house boats, yachts, 18-wheel trailers and all that other big shit that I can't drive. So I crossed out all forty of those. There's a chance that there could be cars in some of them but I don't have all day to be poppin locks. The rest of the garages are your average size. But sixty of them are owned by GM. GM uses those garages to house automobile parts and shit. The remaining twenty were personally owned. It costs approximately seventeen dollars a day to rent these garage units and eighteen of the twenty have been owned for over three years. It's safe to say that if a person can willingly spend twenty racks on just storage then there has to be some good merchandise they have locked up.

The location was important but it was equally as important for me to understand the type of security I would be faced with. According to Google roughly four percent of all Americans actually have alarm systems installed into their detached garages. Attached garages was well over sixty. The odds seemed to be in my favor but I wasn't taking any chances. So before I make this run I have one quick stop to make.

My connect, Navi, lives on the west side of Manhattan. I took that hike to her apartment right around eight in the morning. She was expecting me because I sent her an email last night telling her I was going to visit. Navi used to work at the computer shop across the street from the strip club. Super smart ass bitch. She ended up quitting her job because she cashed out on an mobile application that she created. Most people know it as Groupon.

"Yo Ally! What's shaking, girl?" Navi greeted me.

"What's up, Navi? How's this nerd life treating you?" I joked. Her apartment was set up like a CSI office. Computers and technical shit everywhere.

"Oh you know, just writing programs and hacking firewalls. Same ol same ol." We laughed.

"Look I can't stay long. I got some business I need to handle and I need some help."

"Yea I saw your email. Please spare me on the details just in case the police come looking for me. I don't want to have to lie and say I don't know."

"Cool with me. Long story short I need you to disable an alarm system."

"What kind of alarm system we talking about? 8330? 740?"

"Navi, the fuck is an 8330? I don't know shit about that all that tech shit. I just know it's an alarm system for a garage."

"Ah probably 740. Cool." She went into a closet and came back with a chip with a magnet attached to it.

"This is a an alarm deactivator. Most big time criminals

use these to break into mansions. This should be enough to override the system. Place it on the door near the keypad, turn it on, and wait twenty seconds. Then type in four zeros on the keypad. The garage will open but in two-hundred and forty seconds it will automatically close. So if you're still inside the alarm will sound."

"Ok got it. Twenty seconds then two-hundred and forty seconds. That should be enough time."

"I'll give this to you for the free since I haven't seen you in a while but next time I'm charging." We dapped it up and I headed out to the bus station.

The bus dropped me off right at the corner of the lot. I checked my bag to make sure I had the tools I needed to get the car started. Then I did surveillance. I sat on the curb across the street from the lot for a whole hour. I needed to know what kind of traffic was coming in and out and if there was anyone watching. I also peeped the camera locations. I picked a garage that was out of sight from the camera system.

I pulled my hood down tight and made my way to the garage. Number 103. It was the middle of the morning, around ten and here I was about to attempt to steal a fucking car. But, I read in a book once that if you ever want to commit grand theft do it in the middle of the day. When no one is expecting.

I place the deactivator right in the spot Navi instructed me to and I counted to twenty. One....Two.... this was the longest twenty seconds ... fifteen... eighteen... twenty. Right at twenty, I typed in four zeros and waited. I was kind of hoping that it didn't work so I could have an excuse to leave. But just like Navi said the garage started to open.

Right when the garage got to knee height I knew I hit the fucking jackpot. Three Benz coupes and two fully loaded brand new Range Rovers! I took my chances and hopped in an all-black Range. Car was easily worth ninety grand. Apparently I hit a garage that belonged to a small time dealership because the license plate had "Jim's Luxury Cars" on it. And the fucking keys were in the ignition! I pulled the car out the tight spot careful not to hit anything. Once I got the car out I got out grabbed the deactivator and allowed the garage door to close . Then I took off in the SUV.

I drove the exact speed limit all the way back to the lower end. It took me nearly two hours but I wasn't even thinking about speeding. When I hit 7th Street I busted a quick right to turn down the alleyway then I honked the horn. The pawn shop garage opened and I pulled the car in.

"Ally what the fuck? Where the fuck did you get a brand new fully loaded Range Rover with less than 200 miles on it?" Nino was impressed to say the least.

"I told you I wasn't no rookie."

"No scratches on this bitch. I can easily make some bread off this."

Nino was one of them hella goofy ass hood niggas who had to make a joke about everything but was always about his business.

"Man, as promised, you on the team, fam," his accent kicked in. He's a Midwest type dude that just happened to live in New York.

"Bet. But, more importantly run me my money." I smiled.

Nino cut me ten percent of the sale. After they ran the numbers they came out with a profit of eighty-four grand which left me with little over eight thousand. It's not stripper money but it'll do for now.

5

Back In Action

The human brain often retreats to what is comfortable.

After I got the house payment off for my mom's crib and I dropped enough cash on my landlady I felt a bit more relaxed. I just potentially pulled the greatest crime of my existence and I wasn't even worried. One, because I covered my tracks perfectly when I was in the act and two, there is no evidence left, thanks to Nino.

Before I went home I stopped by my cell phone provider and purchased a replacement phone. They loaded my sim card and all my previous info that I had stored in the cloud before I lost my phone in the subway. I walked out of the store looking down, checking my phone. My voice mailbox was full. Lots of messages from Mama worried sick about me and her house. Apparently she even called my dad, which she never does, because he even called and left me several messages. Then there was a single message from a number I didn't recognize, I played it:

"Ally.. you're probably pissed with me right now but don't be. I was caught up on some shit and was off the grid for a minute. I'll be back. I'll find you."

It was Aaron. Here he goes again with the vague details. He got caught up on some shit? He's off the grid? What does he mean he'll find me? I called the number back but it went to an automated message stating that the number was disconnected. What the fuck?

After a few blocks I was passing by the strip club. It had only been a few days since my suspension but I felt like I was missing something. I've been employed at this same club since I was eighteen. This place was more of my home then my actual home and here I am "grounded" from being there. I couldn't help myself; I walked in.

"Ms. Pink Dollaaaaaa," Draya, one of the bartenders greeted me.

"What's up, girl?" We greeted each other.

"Girl, nothing at all. Same ol. Heard you got suspended on some bullshit tho."

"Yea, I missed a shift. Boss Bitch tripped out and wrote me up. Like I know that bitch is missing hella money without my ass on the floor."

"That's an understatement. We been getting customer complaint calls cause thirsty niggas been coming up in here lookin for yo ass." We laughed.

"Well she said I could come back in two weeks. That's if I feel like dealing with her shady ass."

"It ain't up to her, Mike came in here this morning and got on her ass about production." Mike is the owner of Mike's Gentleman Club. He's also the nigga that hired me years back.

"Mike's the one that approved my suspension," I responded.

"That's not what Mike said this morning. He came up in here asking why your hours were cut and Boss Bitch got to stuttering. I wouldn't be surprised if she didn't call you tonight."

I checked out the scene. During the day it's only a few regulars that come in to get some quality time with their favorite stripper. No real money. I never worked a day shift in my life. I'm always scheduled during prime time hours.

"I gotta run. Do me a favor when you see her; tell her to give me a call. I just got my phone back today."

"Alright, I will."

I had a little cash leftover from that first play with the pawn shop but I knew shit was going to get scarce again real soon. Which meant I needed to go back to plotting. I knew for sure I wasn't about to hit the same place twice especially not in the same week. I would have to be a true dumbass to do some shit like that. I roamed around downtown, thinking. Apparently, the loud noise of the city helps me clear my thoughts and focus. I knew for sure going back to Manhattan is risky but I also knew there wasn't much merchandise in the inner city that would land me some real cash. I had more time this go around to build a better plan. But where to start?

My dad called me for the thirteenth time since I had my phone back so I decided to finally take his call:

"Hello."

"Ally. Where have you been? Got ya old man out here worried sick," he blurted.

"Sorry, Dad. Just been busy this past week." I told a part of the truth.

"Busy or not check in next time."

"Got it, Pops. What's up?" I changed the subject.

"Well, I called you initially because I needed to run some details by you..." he was vague.

"Details? What you talking about?" I paced at the corner.

"Remember when I told you I got caught up with those bookies from Vegas a couple months ago?" He clarified.

"Yea. And I gave you like five racks to pay them off. I remember."

"Well that five thousand was only a partial payment. They're back looking for your old man. Luckily they don't know where I operate but that's the word on the street. I just wanted you to know to keep information at an all-time low."

"Man alright, Pops. Give me a few days and I'll be in touch. I may have a play for you by then. Until then stay low." I warned him.

"Trust me I'm lying lower than a snake right now. Get at me later."

"Alright."

Pops stay in some bullshit. But, this shit here is by far the biggest incident he put himself in. Earlier this year he took a trip out to Vegas. He ended up getting shitty wasted and betting twenty grand against Mayweather in a fight. My dad does some pretty stupid shit but that was just plain retarded. Anyway, he thought he was going to be able to duck the dudes he bet against. But, turns out, they're some big time hustle sharks from New Jersey and were just in Vegas visiting like he was. Long story short, they caught him slipping on the Westside one day and was damn near ready to slice his throat if he didn't put up some money. That's when I came through and saved his bitch ass. Emptied out my entire savings stash just to keep him from seeing his last day on earth. Now I gotta find another way to clear him off their radar. Just another reason for me to make another visit to the pawn shop. Still, I didn't know where to start. I could take my chances Upstate and mess with the foreigners merchandise but I didn't know much about that area. I needed a lead and I needed to find it quick.

As, I paced the cold corners of downtown I got a call from an unknown number. I hesitated in answering as I do with any unknown call. But, something told me to answer it.

"Yo."

"Ally," a familiar voice spoke.

"Who is this?" I wasn't sure and didn't want to be wrong.

"Meet me at the square at seven. Don't be late." Then he hung up.

I was pretty sure that was King. But, why did he call my phone blocked? And a better question is why was he being so short over the phone. He did the exact same thing with his voice message that he left. Something was up.

At seven that night I was sure to be at the exact same corner I first met King at a couple weeks ago. I was bundled up in my fall coat with my Timbs laced loosely finishing the last corner of my Philly sandwich that I had just picked up from Frank's. Best Philly cheesesteaks on this side of town. I was looking for the all black Audi with the unmarked license plate. I knew he was going to show up this time but he was taking forever. I had been waiting ten minutes and there no sign of the Audi. *This better not be a repeat of last time.* It was getting late and the wind chill was starting to get a lot cooler. Just as I bundled up my coat tighter a burgundy Navigator pulled up to the corner and stopped at the light. The passenger window went down and I see King sitting in the passenger seat. He rolled the window down just enough to show his eyes and then he rolled it back up. I took that as my cue to get in the backseat. And that's exactly what I did. When I got in I recognized the driver from the garages that we visited, it was the same super swole dude from before. After I got in, I slid over to the middle seat so that I was in between the both of them. Then the driver took off.

"Aaron what the fuck, man?" was the first and most important question I asked.

He looked over at me with his hoodie on and all I could notice was his light brown eyes and long eyelashes. He smiled. "You just as pretty as I left you."

"Don't be cute with me now." I scowled trying to pretend not to be flattered.

He smiled. "Naw I almost got caught up in a jam and had to lay low for a minute." He explained.

"What kind of jam?" I wanted to know.

"She asks a lot of questions, dog." his homeboy spoke.

I mugged. "What the fuck are you? His lawyer."

King laughed. "This my boy, Loc. This is Ally, lil fine feisty ass," he said pointing to me.

"I see," Loc responded nodding his head. I couldn't tell if he was agreeing that I'm fine or if he was agreeing that I'm feisty.

Loc was literally a big ass body guard type nigga. The type of dude that if he ran up on you, you knew you were about to get yo ass beat. But, it seemed like King ran shit. Loc listened to everything he told him and went with the flow without questioning him. I guess that's how he expected me to operate but I wanted answers.

"Where are y'all taking me?" I asked.

"Here she go with the questions," Loc bitched.

"Chill, dog." King told him. "You going with me, baby. You know I'ma take care of you," he said without turning around to look at me.

I sat back in my seat and accepted defeat for the moment. I was tired and glad to be riding in a car instead of walking so I didn't complain. King made a few calls from a burner phone which made me further question what happened to his cell. He's always low key but today he was particularly short with his phone conversations. We even made a few stops where random dudes brought envelopes to the passenger window and we dipped off without conversation. After about a good forty-five minutes we pulled up to this nice ass house in the South Suburbs. Definitely ducked way off. King dapped up Loc then he opened the passenger door.

"Come on, Ally." I threw Loc the deuces then got out the car. Then Loc took off.

"Where are we?" I asked as we walked up the driveway.

"My house."

"Your house?" I was surprised. This crib had to be worth well over a million, if not more. He entered the garage code into the keypad and the garage door opened exposing his Audi which sat directly in the middle of the garage. The garage was completely bare. Nothing other than his car and the cold cement that covered the ground. I followed him into the back door that he unlocked by entering another code into a keypad. The back door led us directly into a breezeway that was connected to his huge ass modern style kitchen. The place literally looked and smelled brand new like nobody lived here.

"How long have you had this house? It smells brand

new." I was curious.

"I been here for a year now. I'm just never home probably why it still looks new." He finally answered a question.

"Well, let me live here then," I joked.

"If you want you can have it." He seemed serious.

I just looked at him. I couldn't even fathom him being serious so I dismissed his comment immediately. I followed him into the living room where he kicked off his shoes and sat on his large plush sectional. I sat next to him. He turned on the surround sound and played some relaxing music in the background. Then he laid his head back, kicked his feet up, and closed his eyes.

"So what's been going on with you?" he asked with his eyes still closed. I laid my head on his lap and put my feet up on the couch.

"You mean besides getting suspended from work?"

"What? I can't even imagine Mike's running without you."

"Yea well apparently they are having a pretty hard time. I'm waiting on a call from Mike."

He shook his head in agreement.

"Make sure you grab that envelope off the counter." He pointed, switching the subject. "That's the ten grand I owe you from that night you missed at work."

"I didn't think you were serious."

"Yea I know. You don't think I'm serious about a lot of things. But you'll learn. I would have gave it to you a lot sooner but shit got too hot around town."

"Are you going to tell me what happened?" I was hoping I could finally get some answers.

"It's really complicated."

"I'm sure I'll be able to comprehend," I assured him.

"To make a long story short, the Feds tapped into one of my guys phones and arrested him."

"What does that have to do with you though?"

"See in my business if any part of the operation is compromised I shut the whole business down. I can't have myself or any of my other guys catching any heat. The good news is the guy they wrapped up didn't have nothing on him. No cash, no strap, no nothing. Everything is speculation at this point. But he does have to sit in county for a minute because he has a few warrants," he explained calmly all while keeping his eyes closed.

"So where did you go?"

"Out the country. I got a little spot right on the other side of the border in Canada. We ditched all our cell phones and closed up the business for two weeks. Out of sight out of mind while the Feds do their snooping."

"So you think they're done?"

"Hell naw. Them bitches ain't never done but I sent their ass on a wild goose chase. I dropped a few fake bombs to lead them in a different direction while I give all my guys a chance to clean off their hands. Loc working on changing everybody's license plates, changing out burner phones, and getting new ID cards. We'll be back up next week. Until then, I'll be here. I finally get a chance to be at home. It actually feels good."

"And I'm guessing you aren't going to tell me what it is you actually do."

"If I don't tell you then you'll never have to tell a lie," he explained.

I looked up at him. He didn't open his eyes.

• • •

I abruptly woke up to loud banging at the front door. I was still laying on King's lap while we both slept. I immediately hopped up and turned to King who looked worried but wasn't moving as quickly as I was. He got up and opened a closet door nearby. He pulled out an automatic 9 gauge gun then searched in a toolbox for something else. Seconds later the banging continued while King placed a silencer on his gun. Then he motioned me to sit on the floor while he peeked out the front window curtains. He moved so calmly and quietly, making sure not to make too much noise. He then moved over to front door and peeked through the peephole. Then, his face seemed to experience some relief from what he saw on the other side. His demeanor changed as he unlocked the door.

"Dog don't be banging on my damn door like that. Bitch, I thought you were the Feds," King greeted.

"I see. Got the silencer out and everything," the unexpected guest answered.

"I was about to take your life, nigga."

"Well, I called your phone about twenty mothafuckin times."

"I been switching burner phones every hour, " King calmly answered, walking into the kitchen.

"Word on the street is the shop closed down. When the fuck was somebody gone inform me?" he asked.

"Nigga you will be informed when you need to be informed. Your hands not in this pot, my nigga." Aaron responded while pouring a shot of D'ussé into a glass full of ice. Then he poured one for his guest.

"Yea un huh. I see you seem real concerned laid up in here with a bitch," he said, pointing at me as he caught me in the motion of moving from the floor back to the couch.

"Nigga watch yo gotdamn mouth," King replied before I had a chance to.

They walked into the living room. King sat in his original spot and the other guy sat on the matching plush loveseat.

"This is Ally. Ally that's my baby brother, Snoop," he introduced us.

"Oh this you, big bro?" He said shocked. "Excuse my behavior. It's a pleasure to meet you," he said extending his hand.

Snoop was basically a younger version of Aaron. He was just as attractive with the same hair texture and smile as Aaron. Unlike Aaron, he wore his hair in a low cut with a fresh edge line. He's a little taller maybe six-five and he smelled like department store cologne. Like I said, very similar to his brother just less smooth and obviously younger.

"Yea nice to meet you, too" I accepted his gesture but rolled my eyes all at the same time.

"Ooooo, she feisty. Probably a freak huh?" Snoop sat back in his chair and sipped his drink.

"Bitch what I tell you about your mouth," King said to him pointing his gun at Snoop's face.

Snoop laughed. "My bad, dog." Acting as if he was scared but it was obvious that he wasn't. "So what you gon be out here ducked off hiding like a bitch?

"I'm laying low for a few more days. Then the shop goes back up. What shit looking like on your end?"

"Everything Gucci. Except for them few hoe ass niggas

that owe us money out here. I got word that one of them mothafuckas laying low somewhere in Brooklyn. When I find that bitch I'ma personally snap his neck and watch the blood flow out." I listened to their conversation attentively.

"Be careful over there. Niggas might got shooters," King replied.

"Yea, I know. But I'm banking that the old nigga slip up and leave his territory." Snoop shot his drink.

"If you catch that nigga just drop him off in the chop shop and keep ya hands clean, bro."

Snoop nodded. He seemed like the less rational of the two. The type of nigga that acts now then thinks later. King balanced him out. Gave him the direction and he followed.

"Bet that. I'm going upstairs and leave y'all to whatever y'all had going before I got here." He made the slick comment.

King didn't even look up at him. He just laid his head back and closed his eyes all while holding his drink. Snoop went upstairs.

"You don't have to stay here if you don't want," he calmly spoke.

"Where Ima go? I can't go to the club and I don't have a life outside of stripping," I said to him, laying back on his lap. Just like how we were before Snoop intruded.

"Why not?" he questioned.

"Why not what?" Nobody ever asked me that before.

"Why don't you have anything else going other than stripping?" He laid his available hand across my body.

"I don't know. I just don't have anything else to offer the world I guess." I really didn't know the answer.

"You never wanted to do anything else? You grew up

wanting to be a stripper?"

"I grew up in the streets. Brooklyn. Not much to aspire to out there." I answered him honestly.

"The crazy thing about aspirations is that you don't actually have to see it to know that you want it." He spoke all while keeping his eyes closed. "What do you like to do?"

"Make money," I seriously answered.

"Nah… You like having money. What is it that you enjoy doing," he clarified.

"Well... I paint. there's literally nothing in my apartment except my bed and my easels."

"Interesting."

"I mostly paint scenery, places I've seen or want to see. But I'm not that great." I was modest.

"You'll show me one day?"

"If you want." I didn't want to show him.

"I do. I'll remind you." He knew I didn't want to show him.

"Can I ask you something?"

"Of course."

"Are you going to actually answer?" I probed.

He smiled. "No promises, baby."

"What's your plan with me? Why am I here?"

"Ally you already know the answer to that."

"Answer the question."

"So I'm twenty-seven. The last time I was actually interested in a female I was twenty-one. I'm picky as fuck with the type of women I like or pursue."

"And?" I pushed him.

"And I'm pursuing you because you're my type. Strong, smart, independent, sexy. And the fact that there is a 9mm automatic sitting on the table and you haven't asked me why I have it tells me you can handle my lifestyle," he elaborated.

I laughed. "I'm just glad you got the silencer for him because those bitches are loud."

He laughed. "Now I got a question for you."

"What's up" I responded.

"When you gon stop asking me so many damn questions," he clowned.

There's a lot to learn about a person based on their actions. Yes, their words say a lot but what they do truly shows motive. I noticed Aaron didn't speak much. Of course he talked, but he never spoke unless he needed to. He was so careful with his words as if he felt that every word took time and energy and he wanted to minimize his use. I picked up on his protectiveness. The way he took care of things that mattered to him. His "business" and his associates mattered more to him than the actual money that they produced. And even the way he interacted with his brother showed that he valued his relationships the most. We sat up all night discussing the shit we liked and didn't like. For the first time, he actually answered my questions with detail. Aaron explained how he always wanted to be a forensic detective but after he got his degree from Rochester University he became more intrigued by the other side of investigations. The criminal perspective. He explained to me that the type of criminals that can get away with cold blooded murder are some of the smartest most powerful influential people on the planet.

The way he explained it made it seem like an art similar to how I paint. I could tell he'd killed people before just by how calmly he described "the art" process. He seemed skilled like a person with direct experience. I learned a lot about him but more importantly he gave me a chance to open him up.

6

Uncomfortable But Not Worried

When the human brain is uncomfortable it creates physical stress; the trick is to remain calm. Maintain, withstand, and push through.

This past week I spent all my free time, which I had a lot of, with Aaron. I watched him go into full boss mode. He spent most of his time drinking cognac straight and planning his every move. According to him, his whole operation might as well been compromised. He made Loc meet with every last runner on his team to explain the new strategy. King didn't make any personal trips. Most of his runners had no clue what he looked like. His job was to stay low and make all the decisions. Loc managed all the distributors and the distributors managed all the runners. His operation was nothing short of impressive.

After a few days of squatting at Aaron's I decided to face the bullshit that is my life. I needed to get back on my hustle. But, before I hit the city I needed to make a run to drop off the ten grand that Aaron gave me in order to get Pops out of that bullshit with those bookies.

I took the train all the way to Brooklyn. I got off at my usual spot and walked the twelve blocks to my dad's shop. The hood looked the same. Ain't shit changed since the last time I was here. Hustlers still hustling and fiends still buying. When I got to Pop's barbershop the door was locked. Which is strange seeing that it's ten o'clock on a Thursday morning. I banged on the door.

"Pops!" I yelled. No answer.

I went around back to see if the back door was open. It was locked. But, my dad's car was parked behind the shop. How would he get home without his car? I thought then I walked back around to the front and sat on the curb right in front of the door.

"Yo, Ally. Where yo pops been? I need a cut ASAP," one of his loyal customers passed by.

"When the last time you seen him?" I asked.

"It had to be a few days now. I came by yesterday to get some DVDs from the bootleg man and nobody was here," he answered.

I stood up from the curb. "Alright I appreciate the info. I'll find him," I assured his customer.

I walked through the windy streets of Brooklyn for miles. I was headed for my pop's crib but I didn't want to take the bus just in case I ran into somebody that could help me find him. I saw a few folk around the way and asked about him but, nobody had seen him in at least three days.

When I finally made it to his brownstone I banged on the door. When my fists weren't sufficient enough I started kicking. I guess I must have been too loud because his immediate next door neighbor came out.

"You looking for Larry?" an elderly lady asked.

"Yea have you seen him?" I responded.

She pulled her robe tight around her body as she walked closer over to me then she whispered, "I saw him get in the car with two men on Tuesday night. Hadn't seen him since," she told me.

"What kind of car?" I probed.

"One of those expensive SUV things. He didn't look like he wanted to go with them."

I stood there for a second picturing the scene in my mind.

"Thanks," I told the lady and then I took off.

"I hope you find him," she yelled at me from halfway down the street.

I wasn't worried. I was uncomfortable but I definitely wasn't worried. I'm pretty sure those bookies picked him up. And my guess is instead of catching a case for a dead body they would rather catch their money. All I had to do was wait for that phone call. He always called me. I knew he would call. I wasn't worried.

7

Busy People

Some things are just hard to explain...

I read in a book once that the body merely exists in the world but the mind and the soul are of the world. I always heavily relied on my body for steady cash but when shit got tough my mind was what I used to overcome. I have never been too weak, mentally, to overcome adversity.

This morning I woke up in my cold electric less apartment. I didn't pay my electricity bill this month. I'm saving all my cash for my pops, for whenever he calls. I slept in a full sweat suit, two pairs of socks, and a beanie under three thick blankets. The winter was settling in and the cement floors and brick walls of my apartment were making it painfully clear.

Aaron: Where are you?

He texted me in the middle of the night but I didn't reply until early this morning.

Me: Home. What's up?

Aaron: I'm coming to get you. I miss you.

He wrote back immediately. I was relieved he was coming to pick me up because right before he replied I realized there was no food in my fridge. And Aaron always has food at his place. I put on some jeans and my Timbs then pulled my hair back in a ponytail. Then I brushed my teeth in the dark and washed my face. Then, I packed a small duffle bag just in case I'm gone long. I waited another twenty minutes then Aaron texted me prompting me to come downstairs.

When I got in the car Loc was driving, Aaron was in the passenger seat and Snoop was in the backseat behind him.

"Oh look who it is. Lil miss feisty herself," Snoop joked. Loc Laughed.

I mugged.

"Bet she ask about twenty-seven different questions before we get out the car," Loc added to Snoop's slug. They laughed in unison.

"You can eat a dick," I replied. They continued to laugh.

"Yo cool out on my baby, G," King ordered without looking up from his phone.

"Where to?" Loc asked, changing the subject.

"Drop me off at the low end. Got some unfinished business to tend to," Snoop answered as Loc drove off.

"Fuck you got going?" King asked.

"Collecting old debts," Snoop replied.

"Yeah alright, dog," King Dismissed.

We drove Snoop to his location. I sat back and enjoyed every second of the centralized heat. King, Snoop, and Loc discussed business as usual.

"So all the right people are in the right places. They're

just waiting for the product," Loc spoke.

"I'm cooking on that right as we speak. We just need to do an exchange at eleven tonight," King answered.

"The full shipment?"

"The entire thing. That's why we need Snoop and his boys on point. Just in case shit get a little rough," King replied.

"No can do, Boss Man," Snoop shook his head.

"Fuck you mean no?!" King raised his voice.

"I'm busy tonight," Snoop nonchalantly answered, disregarding King's anger.

"Personally, I don't give a fuck if you got dinner planned with Obama. Yo ass gone look out tonight at the garages in Manhattan," his voice calmed as he made his final demand.

"I'll see what I can do," Snoop answered as we pulled up to his stop.

"Ain't nothing to see about. Tonight at eleven, lil ass nigga. Or Ima come find yo ass," King put his foot down and Snoop got out the car.

Everything about Aaron was hardcore. From the way he ran his crew to how he handled his relationships. You could always tell he has a heart but you won't ever be able to run him over. He's mentally strong which was a plus because his physical may lead you to think otherwise. His six-four frame was tall, slender and fit, but he clearly wasn't the biggest man in the room. Regardless, when he spoke people listened and obeyed his commands. He never took no for an answer and, quite frankly, most people are scared to tell him no. Well, except for Snoop.

"I need you to make a run for me," King told Loc. "But, in the meantime, drop us off at the Square," he pointed to me.

Loc dropped us off right in front of the Philly shop on Times Avenue. My stomach instantly started to growl from the scent of beef on the grill but Aaron had other plans for us. I followed him to a private restaurant just a few doors down from where we were dropped off. We walked up to the small Italian restaurant where the owner seemed to know Aaron quite well. We were seated at a booth near the bar and immediately greeted with cold water and warm garlic bread.

"I've never even noticed this place before," I spoke while I buttered my bread.

"I told you I'm putting you on new things," he answered, ignoring the delicious gourmet bread while he texted on his phone.

"You literally been on your phone all day," I pointed out.

He looked up at me. "Man, I know. Today is kind of important for me. Just making sure shit straight." He sat his phone on the table.

"Yeah, I've noticed. You got everybody running around."

"It's all strategic, baby. What's up with you though? Why you been hiding from me?" he asked.

"Just...busy. You know," I vaguely answered.

He peered his eyes at me as if he knew I was telling a bold face lie. The waitress walked up and took our orders then we went back to our conversation.

"Busy huh?" he probed.

"Yeah." I didn't look at him when I replied.

"You know busy people tend to only tell people they're actually busy without an explanation if they don't want to be bothered or they're lying. So which one are you?" he dug deep.

"Neither. I just got a dilemma on my hands," I opened up.

"I'm really insulted that you choose not to communicate with me," he joked but was a tiny bit serious.

"If it makes you feel better I don't communicate with anyone much," I countered.

"That does not make me feel better. Tell me," he pushed.

"I just been waiting for this really important call from my pops."

"Everything cool?" he genuinely asked.

"That's why I'm waiting on his call. I haven't heard from him in a week and he isn't at home."

This time when he peered his eyes at me he could tell I was telling the truth. He could also tell from the change in my tone and my demeanor that I didn't want to say much more. He nodded his head confirming that he picked up on my non-verbal cues. "He'll call," he assured me.

We ate our dishes that were finely prepared by the chef. I had a triple layered lasagna that was so good I didn't even notice what Aaron ordered. Once we were done we got up and walked toward the door. Aaron threw the owner the deuces and we left without paying.

"How do you have a plug everywhere you go?" I was curious.

"I'm the plug," he smiled. His dimples showed.

"Look Ima have Loc drop you off at the house. We have some business to handle," he said, checking his watch.

"Nah that's cool. I'm back on the schedule at Mike's. I really should run. I have to be on stage in an hour."

He raised his eyebrows at me in concern. "You gon be alright?"

"Yeah, it's only a few blocks from here."

"What time you get off?"

"Like two."

"You're coming home with me. I'll pick you up," he ordered.

"Cool with me."

We hugged then he kissed my forehead and touched my face. We separated ourselves from one another and Aaron got in the car with Loc and I took off the other way headed towards Mike's.

8

Welcome Back

Rule number 1: Don't forget to get the money.

10:30pm

"Coming to the stage after an over extended vacation, everybody's favorite thick stallion, the lady that got the thrills to pay the bills… Ms. Pinkkk Dollaaa!"

"It's ya birthday, bad bitch contest, you in first place." 2 Chainz filled the speakers.

I walked out on the stage and stood front and center in my leather pink boy shorts and matching bikini top. My booty swallowed my shorts making them look more like a thong and my top was two sizes too small for my 34F tits.

Dudes rushed the stage waiting to see what kind of tricks I had up my sleeve. I strolled over to the very front of the stage and watched men throw singles at just the sight of my body. Now to make them throw those twenties. I signaled the DJ to switch the song. As soon as Ginuwine's voice hit the speakers to his classic hit "Pony," my ass hit the stage, literally, in a split. I bounced my ass up and down making it jiggle against the stage. Men started putting five dollar bills in my pink garter. But, I needed to see bigger bills. I flipped upside down with my head hanging off the stage and my legs in the air, exposing my pussy print. Then, I raised myself up on my hands into a handstand on the very edge of the stage and made my ass clap to the beat. I started to see the tens come out. Still in a handstand, I walked my hands over to the pole then wrapped my legs around it pulling my torso up off the ground. Then, I slid my top off, exposing my titties and my nipple rings. That's when the twenties hit the stage. But, I wanted to see more. Still hanging upside down, I grabbed both of my tits with each of my hands and licked my nipples until they were rock solid. The crowd howled like a pack of wild dogs. Once I saw the hundreds come out I knew I had em right where I wanted them. The song switched, meaning I had less that four minutes to milk these mothafuckas for every last dollar in their pockets before my two song minimum was up. I flipped upright and climbed to the top of the pole slowly using just my arms, allowing my legs to dangle as I freely clapped my thick ass. When I got to the top I grabbed the bars on the ceiling and spread my legs into a split. Then, I threw my legs around the pole and slid back down full speed upside down, stopping right before I hit the ground. Then, I flipped over into a split still holding the pole balancing myself in mid-air popping my booty to the beat. Then, I dropped allowing my body to bounce freely against the stage as men fought over who was going to place the most money in my tiny shorts.

At 10:42 pm I walked off the stage with four buckets full of money.

I changed out of my stage outfit into my lap dance fit which was a completely lace skin tight jumpsuit. I placed pink tape over my nipples to make sure my rings didn't get stuck in the lace. My titties and ass were completely visible. Once my look was complete, I walked out to the floor to make more money.

"Ms. Pink Dolla. Glad to see you're back." Mike met me directly outside of the locker room doors.

I laughed. "I bet," I responded as I thought about all the shit Layla and I had been talking about the club missing money.

Mike went back to sipping his gin and looking at asses and I went back to work. I had been out of work for a little over two weeks and needed to catch up on my money. I walked through the club turning down lap dance requests left and right. I was looking for a certain type of customer. That kind of man or woman that you knew was ready to drop their whole week's paycheck on some hypothetical pussy. I leave them twenty dollar lap dances for the basic hoes. All money ain't good money especially if it don't involve a few commas.

At 11:01pm I made my way to VIP after I grabbed a drink from the bar.

"Oh look who it is, Pink Dolla," a familiar face from the New York Giants greeted me.

"You been looking for me?" I asked, noticing the bankroll in his pocket.

"I saw your stage performance. I was wondering if I can get a personal version of that," he said, sitting back in his seat.

I sat my drink down and made my disclaimer "I must warn you that I am Ms. Pink Dolla and I am a certified dick pleaser. Please proceed with caution" then, I gave him what he asked for.

My normal policy is to meet the two song requirement, get my money, and move on. But, this football player was generously throwing hundreds. I would have been a fool to move around after two songs. He caressed my body while I teased him for damn near thirty minutes before he started running low on hundreds and started throwing twenties.

"You should come home with me," he offered. What would have been a tempting offer to anyone else seeing that he was fine, built, and paid, was just a turnoff for me.

"Maybe another time." I politely rejected him. I definitely didn't want to offend him but I wanted it to be clear that I was not going to fuck him.

"You should definitely think about it. I'll treat you right," he made generous promises while flashing his pretty smile.

I smiled. "I'll consider it," I lied. I wasn't going to consider shit. I politely gathered my money and moved on.

My night continued on like that for the next three hours. I danced for some high roller, acquired a couple thousand, he offered to take me home, I turn him down and move on. At the end of the night I counted my money. A couple hundred dollars shy of eleven racks. Pretty successful night if I say so myself.

"Oh shit, Ally! You racked up tonight girl," Toya greeted me.

I laughed. "Only on some light boss shit," I bragged.

"These thirsty ass niggas was begging for your ass to come back. Getting on my last damn nerves," she added.

"Tell me about it. That's all I heard all night. But, I listened and gladly took their money." We laughed.

"So what's with you and that fine ass dude you went out

with that one time?" She reminded me that I haven't updated her on my life.

"We been kicking it." I was modest.

"Oh shit!" She was extra. "Finally, you getting dicked down. That's why you been smiling more."

"Actually we haven't been fucking, nosey ass," I responded.

"The fuck you been doing then?"

"I don't know. He just been trying to get to know me. You know, kicking it."

"Damn you got a good one on the first try," she laughed. "Well I'm about to get back out here and try to get some of that Pink Dolla money." We both laughed.

I checked my phone:

Aaron: I'm outside

Me: Coming now

I made my drop at the front office then, I pulled my hood over my head and went back to the brisk streets of New York. Aaron was sitting in front of the club in his Audi coup. I got in and he pulled off. He was on the phone:

"Nah bitch you was late and I specifically told you to be on time. I don't wanna hear none of those weak ass excuses." He was going off on somebody.

"... yeah, dog alright. Get off my line." He hung up. "That nigga Snoop gone make me lay his ass out." He started our conversation.

"You always say that and never do." I disregarded his statement.

"Man. I know. One day tho." He shook his head. "So on a

scale of one to ten how thirsty were your customers tonight?" he asked.

"Hmm.. I'ma say a solid nine hundred," I laughed.

"I bet. Fine ass." He looked over at me.

"How'd your exchange go?" I air quoted exchange.

"Everything Gucci." He made the okay sign with his right hand.

"That's good."

"I got you something. It's in the backseat," he said to me randomly.

"Who me?"

He looked around the car to see if there was anyone else he could possibly be talking to. "Yeah you," he laughed.

I looked in the backseat to see what he was talking about. I grabbed the shopping bag and pulled out an all red North Face jacket.

"It's made out of wool and leather. You know some extra warm ass shit," he explained.

"Wow. That's so nice of you." I couldn't think of shit to say.

"It's just a jacket. But, it's getting cold out here so you might as well get fresh."

I smiled. I was appreciative. I literally cannot remember the last time somebody gave me a gift. A thoughtful useful gift at that. Aaron drove us the thirty minutes to his crib while he talked on the phone. For it to be almost three in the morning he got a lot of phone calls. The craziest thing about Aaron was that he never received personal calls only business.

Once we parked and got in the house I placed my bag down in the living room and Aaron turned his phone off.

"Everything should be good now, no need for me to keep answering calls," he said, walking into the kitchen.

He pulled out some day old leftover Chinese food and warmed it up in the microwave still in the box. Once it signaled that it was ready he handed me a plastic fork and we ate from the box at his dining room table.

"Something about tonight felt weird," I confessed.

Aaron raised his eyebrow. "Elaborate," he requested.

"Me... at Mike's. It didn't feel normal. I felt like a professional. I felt overly confident and assured. I felt like I was too good to be there," I explained.

He smiled. "That's good. That sounds like growth to me."

"How'd you do that?" I asked him.

"Do what?" His forehead wrinkled in confusion.

"Rub off on me. Convince me that there was more out there than the strip club," I clarified.

"I didn't do shit. You did that. I just simply helped you out that one track thinking mode you were stuck in. The real question now is are you ready to take action?"

I shook my head in uncertainty.

"You'll get there," he assured me.

Aaron's presence made me comfortable, hopeful, and happy. I always took everything he said into consideration without question.

I leaned over bringing my face right next to his then I kissed his cheek. He turned his head facing me then I kissed his lips. He embraced my gestures and kissed me back. Passionately. Like he had been waiting a while for this very moment. I wrapped my arms around his neck and he grabbed me by my waist, pulling me into his lap. His lips were soft and supple. He interlaced his tongue occasionally between our motions, enhancing our passion. His hands caressed my skin involving my entire body in the experience.

He picked me up and walked us to his room. He was gentle and careful but sexy and confident all at the same time. He pushed open the door with his foot, careful to not remove his hands that he had firmly gripped around my ass.

His room was much more chilly than the rest of the house. This was only the second time I had ever been in his room and my first time in his bed. All the other nights I stayed over he left me to sleep comfortably in his guest room. His California King bed was firm and plush, covered in expensive red sheets accompanied with a warm comforter. He laid me across the bed then, he stood up and took his shirt off. His entire chest, stomach, arms, and back were covered in tattoos. There had to be at least a hundred different designs inked on his strong slender frame. His abs showed through the ink and his arms and chest were chiseled to perfection. My mouth dropped open when he took off his sweats and exposed his dick print. It looked like he had a water bottle stuffed in his boxer briefs. He had no more tattoos on his body. His entire lower body, hands, and face were completely free of ink.

I then did what I do best: strip out of my clothes. After I pulled off my hoodie and sweats I was sitting on the bed in a pink push up bra and matching thong. Freshly shaved and oiled thanks to my job.

"You show me everything and I'll show you everything gripping his dick.

I pulled off my bra slowly and seductively, exposing my bare tits. He licked his lips. I slipped off my thong and ran my fingers over my already wet lips. I watched his manhood rise. As promised, he got completely nude, showing off his long dick. His tip was significantly thicker than his shaft; perfect for clitoris arousal.

He then crawled across the bed on his hands and knees, lion style, toward me and forcefully dragged me by my legs placing my entire body under his. He kissed my neck then licked my nipples until I started to moan, digging my fingers in his back. Right when he thought I was soaked enough he pulled me by my waist and put himself inside with just his left hand. He fit snugly. I moaned.

"Open up, baby," he commanded.

I listened, relaxed, and brought my legs back closer to my torso. He stroked my wet tight pussy with his thick dick until I started moaning his name. He held both of my titties in each of his hands as he pulled himself in deeper. He closed his eyes and enjoyed every minute of my wetness. I came on his dick leaving the sex scene even more wet than before. He flipped me over and gripped my ass while I put a deep arch in my back and he went back in. This time faster and harder. I could feel my ass and my tits bouncing back and forth with every stroke. His stroke was distinct; every time he drew back he pulled out his tip just enough to hit the hood of my clit then, then he went back in and repeated over and over again until I yelled "I'm cuming."

I busted again and then moments after me he pulled out and covered my entire ass in creamy sauce. I laid out flat on my stomach from exhaustion and he laid out on his back.

9

Basic Operations

Don't ask the question if you're not ready for the answer.

There's something to be said about the physical interaction between two people. Interconnection between two like souls can be magical, an experience beyond our world. The interesting part is when mutual feelings exist compassion is created and companion hormones are expelled. But, when mutual feelings don't exist it is merely a physical activity rather than a spiritual journey. Aaron took me on a spiritual extravaganza and I have absolutely no complaints.

That morning I woke up in Aaron's bed. My normal wake up routine includes me dragging and hanging around under the covers for at least forty-five minutes before even attempting to get up but not today. I was wide awake at seven, which was amazing seeing that I had only went to sleep a few hours ago. Aaron wasn't lying next to me. His side of the bed was still warm so I knew he was here but he wasn't physically in the bed. I got up and pulled a long sleeve oversized tee shirt out of one of his drawers and covered my nude body. The room was clean. My clothes weren't scattered across the room and a condom wrapper wasn't inconveniently laying in a random place. This was definitely not your typical "morning after" setup. I took a left out of Aaron's master bedroom and walked down a wide short hallway. At the end of the hallway was an office and there were voices coming from the room. I eavesdropped.

"I told you to drop that mothafucka off at the chop shop." It was King's voice.

"I much rather keep him locked up until I get what I want," a voice spoke through the speakerphone. I'm pretty sure it was Snoop.

"That shit keeping you occupied for no reason. That's petty money, bro," King replied.

"This one is personal. I'll link up with you a little later. I got some business to tend to."

"Bet." Then they hung up.

I conveniently appeared from around the corner once their conversation was over.

"Good morning." My voice was raspy and quiet.

"Come here." Aaron opened his arms inviting me to sit on his lap. I accepted his gesture.

"I feel like I should be cooking you breakfast right now because of all that good dick last night," I clowned. He laughed. He was still in his pajama pants, wearing no shirt.

"Shit then I feel like I should be taking you shopping cause that shit right there..." he over exaggerated, pointing down between my legs.

"I might take you up on that offer," I joked back.

"Please do. Whenever you're ready, baby," he confirmed while gripping my body. Then he grabbed his phone to check a text.

"But on a more serious note, Can you take me home? I'm out of clothes."

"Take you home? Naw, you are at home." He was firm.

I just stared at him. He didn't look up from his phone. He didn't make a facial expression.

"You can go to the city to get all your stuff. Then let your landlord know you not coming back." He was serious.

"I can't move here. This is way too far from the club. It'll take me two hours to get there on the bus." I was thinking logically.

"I'll buy you a car. What other excuses you got?" He took a break from looking at his phone to look at me directly in my eyes. He was not joking.

"Fine. I guess I need to get dressed and make moves." I was sarcastic.

"That's a good idea," he matched my sarcasm. "Loc's downstairs. He'll take you wherever you need to go. He has money on him too if you need cash." Then he kissed my forehead and went back to work.

After I changed and halfway put myself together, I rode with Loc to my side of town. He was quiet for the most part. He blasted Fabolous' latest project and mouthed the words to his favorite parts. I chilled and enjoyed the ride.

"Why you always so chill?" Loc turned his music down for a second.

I looked over at him. "I don't know. Nothing really to be turnt about."

"I'm just saying. We make business transactions in front of you, plot on illegal shit all the time, and we clown you and your facial expression never changes. What's up with that?" This is the most I've ever heard Loc speak.

I laughed. "I guess I'm just chill like that." I had no explanation to offer him.

He nodded.

"I got a question though." I took my opportunity.

"Of course you do," he clowned.

"What is it that y'all do?"

"You mean King ain't told you?" He shook his head.

"Nah. I just assume y'all push major drugs but what kind. Cocaine, heroine?"

"Nah, nah, we don't fuck around with that baby shit. We're in the counterfeit business. We manufacture counterfeit bills and sell em to anybody that want em. Mostly politicians are our customers. They buy millions of dollars' worth of counterfeit bills to use for bribes and shit," he explained. I was blown.

"Damn and that's major business for y'all?"

He laughed. "We run this shit. Nobody on this side of the hemisphere push more counterfeit bills than us. We literally have clientele all over the world."

"But I thought y'all had runners. Pushing shit in the streets."

"We do. But our runners wear business suits. We official with this shit."

"That's wild, yo. If you got caught up do you know what kind of bid that would run you?" I asked.

"Federal felony counts of grand larceny and tax evasion. Not to mention several counts of terrorism charges for supplying other countries. Oh and the murders. Can't forget the body count," Loc rambled off. He was fully aware of the crimes he committed daily but he seemed completely unbothered.

"King is smart. He never sleeps, he's always working and he's always five steps ahead of any of us. I'm in good hands," he assured me.

"Now forget I told you any of that," he commanded and I nodded in agreement.

When I got to my studio apartment I ran inside and packed a few bags. Loc came up with me to help. On the way up to my floor I noticed Loc checking the place out. He seemed surprised.

"Damn, Pinky I thought you would be living a little bit better than this seeing that you made all that money at Mike's." He called me Pinky short for my stage name. I hated it.

"Well you thought wrong." I ignored him.

"You painted these?" He awed at my art work that lay against the walls in my apartment.

"Every last one. Speaking of, we need to take those too." He started carefully moving my art pieces down to his SUV.

I packed my minimal wardrobe into a single moving trunk and closed it tight. Then roamed around to see if there was anything of value that I needed. Besides my laptop there was nothing that I just had to take with me.

"Ally what's going on?" Ms. Mack barged in, noticing me packing.

"Moving." I was blunt.

"You do know I'm going to need two months' notice and all my back rent before you just up and leave." She gave me so much attitude. Just as she finished her sentence Loc's overbearing figure appeared.

She turned and faced him.

"What's the total?" He asked without me even prompting him.

"Well... It's at least six or seven thousand," she fumbled with her words.

He pulled out a stack of hundreds banded together with a rubber band.

"This should cover it." He handed the money to her then inched past to continue packing up the SUV.

"Well... She'll still need to put in a two month notice."

"Lady, that should cover everything. Don't be greedy now," Loc demanded as he carried my easel down the hallway.

Once Loc was well out of sight she spoke. "So I see you found yourself a drug dealer boyfriend to get you out the hood." She was salty.

"Yep, sure whatever you think."

I went along with her story so she could feel better about herself. Then she left to count the stack of hundreds. I placed my laptop backpack on my back then attempted to drag the trunk as far down the hallway as I could before Loc intercepted and carried it with ease to the curb.

Once everything was safely packed and loaded in the SUV, we headed out. I didn't look back not even once on that shabby studio apartment. At one point in my life that apartment meant everything to me, but today it was merely a piece of my past. I had grown beyond the four wall confinement that I called home for so many years.

When we got back to my new home Loc unloaded the car and placed all my personal items in one of the guest rooms downstairs. He placed my easel, supplies, and artwork in the garage in an empty space. The Audi was gone which meant

Aaron was out running the streets. Snoop was in the living room smoking and rolling a blunt at the same time.

"So I see you permanent now huh, Pinky," Snoop commented. Apparently he and Loc decided on my nickname together.

"Definitely looks that way," I responded, sitting on the couch with a cold bottle of water that I grabbed from the fridge.

"Never thought I'd see the day my big bro wife a woman." He spoke to himself as he sealed his blunt with his tongue. I didn't entertain him.

"You smoke?" He asked while he lit up.

I nodded. Loc sat down and turned on the TV. Then we all got high together. Snoop talked the entire time about any and everything. He went from asking us what kind of Audemars he should purchase to asking how we felt about a bitch he was trying to smash. I added my two cents when asked but I mostly just observed Loc and Snoop's interaction.

"Just got a text from the boss man. Got a run to make. Snoop you rollin?" Loc stood up and got himself together to make his run.

"I'm down, bro." Snoop finished the blunt.

"What about me?" I spoke up.

"What about you?" Snoop replied.

"Y'all can't just leave me here by myself all day." I stood my ground.

"Nah, Pinky you can't roll with us. We got business to handle," Loc confirmed.

"I'm down. I ain't staying here by myself." I was firm.

"Man just let her ride. She quiet any way." Snoop didn't

care.

"Just make sure King know that this was your call," Loc added while picking up his keys and heading out the garage. I followed behind him.

"Man, I ain't worried bout King." Snoop was honest.

I rode in the backseat behind Loc and Snoop sat in the passenger seat. He lit another blunt for our hour long drive to Manhattan. I became familiar with this route to the white garages. So familiar that I could make this run solo with ease. When we pulled up Loc parked the car and they both hopped out.

"Stay here, Pinky," Loc spoke as if he thought I was planning on going somewhere.

Snoop unlocked the latch on the garage and Loc lifted up the heavy metal door. Then, Snoop disarmed the alarm system. Similar to the system I had to hot wire when I stole the Range a couple months back. There had to be at least sixty different unmarked crates inside. Loc used a dolly and rolled one crate out the garage and moved it to the trunk. Snoop seemed to be checking an inventory sheet and marking notes with a pen. Then, he hung the clipboard that he was holding back up and let down the garage door. Locking it securely. Then, they both got back in the car.

"He only requested one load this time?" Snoop confirmed with Loc.

"Yea. One full load and that was it," Loc stated. Snoop nodded. And we took off. We drove for another hour or so back toward the city. We ended up dead in the center of downtown on Congress Street. We pulled around back of the Commissioner building and Loc parked the car. Then he made a call.

"Drop landed. Prepare for unload." Then he waited a few minutes for the gates to an alley way to open and pulled in. Once inside, Snoop and Loc checked the bullet count in their firearms and adjusted accordingly. They both hopped out with their tool on their hip. Snoop made the transaction with a white gentleman in a gray suit and Loc unloaded the shipment. Snoop shook hands. And they both got back in the car.

"Do me a favor, Pinky. Grab that machine on the floor next to your feet," Snoop asked. I looked down and picked up the light weight machine.

"Turn it on and run this through. Let me know the final count." He handed me a stack of cash.

I turned on the machine, inserted the bills facing downward into the machine, then pressed run.

"Fifty thousand," I responded.

"Perfect. Place the money in a blue band and drop it in the money bag." I followed instructions, banding the money together, placing the correct label on the band matching the dollar amount, and dropping the band into the large money bag in the seat behind me. Then I placed the money counting machine back on the floor.

"Now what?" I asked. I was starved.

"After we make this deposit we can chill until the next run," Loc confirmed. I was patient.

We made our last stop at an unmarked location. We waited twenty minutes and then a Brink's truck pulled up. We handed over our money bag and in turn we received a receipt. And just like that we were completely free of any contraband.

Ally

10

Meet Travis

Travis. In English, this name is meant to symbolize
crossing or crossroads.

I spent most of my days hustlin. Gettin money anyway I can. Stacking my paper day after day. I never knew when I was going to need to cash out.

Typically on Saturday mornings I would wake up to an empty bed. Aaron was up and gone running the streets with Loc. His house, our house I should say, always felt warm and comfortable. This particular morning I walked around in soft pink lace boy shorts accompanied with a fit white crop top and no bra. I knew no one was home and that Aaron wouldn't be back for hours. I finally had a weekend day off from the club and wanted to enjoy every second of it. A few weeks back Aaron gave Loc the task of completely redecorating the guest bedroom downstairs into my personal art studio. A fairly large sized room with two master easels, a full painting station with every color palette available and a small desk in the corner used for stencil and mock designs. The entire left side of the room had stacks of completed paintings resting against the wall covering half of the two bay windows that exposed the view of the backyard. If I painted between the sunrise and right about noon I had the great natural lighting. It was perfect.

Aaron had this weird fascination with gourmet coffee and got me hooked on having a cup every morning. I stood in my studio, in my underclothes, sipping coffee and painting at eight in the morning. My sufficient replacement for Saturday morning cartoons.

I paced back and forth down the length of the room trying to get enough inspiration to complete my latest piece.

"Need some help," a voice spoke from the doorway, startling me. I damn near spilled my coffee before I had the chance to compose myself. It was Snoop.

"Actually I'm good," I was snotty with my response.

He smiled. Then he took a quick glance at my curves then he refocused his attention to my easel.

"What is it?" he asked.

I gave him a sharp look for being all up in my business then I opened up a little. "It's my depiction of the Nightlife. It's what people see when they are wasted." I smiled behind my coffee mug. He laughed.

"Oh I think I see it. Looks like a blurred bathroom stall," he noticed.

I nodded in agreement. "I probably should go put some clothes on." I excused myself then eased past Snoop and went upstairs.

I threw on some leggings over my boy shorts and when I came back down Snoop was sitting on the couch rolling a blunt per usual.

"Why are you here?" I asked him as I fumbled around the

kitchen.

"You don't want me around, Pinky?" his voice was deep and firm.

"I never said that."

"So then what's the issue?" he was curious.

"I mean I was chillin just fine this morning without any company."

"Honestly, you could have kept chillin. Because that's exactly what I'm about to do," he said, propping his feet up and sparking the blunt.

I joined him in the living room. Most days Snoop wore all black. Normally black cargos, black hoodie under his black North Face, and black Timbs.

"Why you always wearing all black?" I asked him as he passed the spliff.

"It's my favorite color." He was forward. "Why you always wearing pink?" he countered my question.

"I don't."

"Yes you do. All the time. You wear pink every day. You had on a pink sweat suit on Thursday. You work out in pink Nikes. You always carry that pink Puma bag every day." He was specific.

"Well... I'm not wearing pink right now," I said while passing.

He paused to clear his lungs of smoke. "You got on pink panties," he laughed.

I laughed. He had a point.

"Not to mention you wear pink every single night at the strip club."

I turned my attention to his remark. "How'd you know that?" I never wore my work clothes outside of the club.

He smiled. Then, he looked at me with his eyebrows raised like he was confused that I even asked him that question. "Ms. Pink Dolla Bill," he said, raising his free hand to gesture that he clearly knew my stage name.

I was surprised. I'm not sure why. I think it was more of a surprise that he clearly was familiar with my occupation but I never told him about my job and I'm pretty sure Aaron doesn't talk about it with him.

"Why you look so surprised?" his question was genuine.

"I mean... I just didn't know you knew where I worked," I responded.

He laughed. "Are you serious? Mike's is literally my favorite club. I been going there since I was like sixteen." He found the whole situation comical.

"Mike really should work on that letting minors in bullshit."

"Mike don't give a fuck. As long as you got that dub to get in the door he'll let a toddler in that bitch." He wasn't lying.

"So I'm curious now..." I swiped my bang behind my ear as I spoke.

"You wanna know if I ever seen you naked?" He looked up from his phone at me. I nodded.

"Of course. Plenty of times. Too many times." I was literally embarrassed.

"Wow." I didn't know what to say.

"Don't stop talking now. What you curious about Pinky?" He played with my emotions.

He was right I wanted to know more. "Why haven't I ever danced for you?" I probed.

"I don't know. That's a good question." He paused and

thought about it. "I think it's because you're so popular. You know. Dudes be all on you all night long. Trust me I thought about it a few times but I ain't the thirsty type."

"I don't get that much play." I was modest.

"You funny, Pinky" he smiled. "But it's definitely a fantasy of mine." He looked away with that statement.

This was my first time actually talking to Snoop about anything personal. He was so cool. Just like Aaron. He was laid back. Honest and forward.

"So what do you have planned for today?" I changed the subject.

"I don't know. I made all my drops earlier this morning and I don't have shit scheduled to move again until way later tonight. So I guess nothing is planned. What about you?"

"Same. I'm off today with nothing planned." I responded.

"King and Loc had a play out in Connecticut. They not coming back until at least 2am. The operation moving in slow motion today."

He was right. Everything was happening so slow. It was barely nine but it felt like I been up all day.

"I know one thing tho, them munchies definitely setting in." He looked over at me for confirmation.

I nodded in agreement. "If I was in the city I would hit 43rd and grab brunch," I thought out loud.

He finished the blunt and put it out then he said, "Go put a bra on so we can go." He touched my nipple through my shirt with his finger tip then got up from the couch. Snoop was an asshole but yet cool all at the same time. I took his advice and put on a bra under my tee shirt then put on my North Face and boots.

Snoop drove us in his white Range Rover out of the burbs

into the city. The snow had finally settled from a long blizzardy night. Traffic was light but it was still a good forty minute drive before we reached 43rd Street.

"So I have another question…" I reintroduced our conversation from earlier.

"Shoot."

"You never told me what you think."

"What you mean?" he asked for clarification.

"You told me about how you think every other guy in the club views me but you never told me what you thought," I expanded my question.

"I think the same thing they think," he was vague. I just looked over at him to see if his facial expression changed. It didn't. "You're gorgeous. But you knew that already," he added.

"That's not what everybody thinks about me. Most of them think I'm fine because my ass is fat and my titties are big. I'm not fooled."

"I mean… you are fine. That's true too. But, you got a pretty ass face too." I was flattered.

I blushed but I covered it by turning my face toward the window. "Thank you."

Snoop laughed. "I can't believe you're shy. That's crazy, I would have never guessed that one."

"There's a lot you don't know about me."

"That's unfortunate." He shook his head.

"What?"

"I'm just thinking. King and I look real similar. If I knew you liked street niggas I would have been shot that shot." He dropped his hints. I didn't probe further. I could have but that was one door I didn't need to open.

100

"What do you mean you didn't know I liked street niggas? What do you think I like?"

"I don't know. You look like the kind of jawn that only like foreign dudes or some other saddity type shit."

"Saddity? Wow." He was way off.

"Yea I know you're not now."

We continued our ride into the city. He left his wallet open in the center console and I took a glance at his driver's license.

"Travis," I laughed.

"Man give me that." He snatched his wallet back. "Mind your business, Pinky," he scowled.

"Oh my bad, Travis. It won't happen again." I was petty. He didn't think it was funny.

By the time we got to the brunch spot on 43rd I felt like I knew a whole new person than from who I originally met that first night Snoop and I were introduced. He was the same kind of gentleman as his brother. He made sure to escort me to our seats, hovering close to me for protection. He took my jacket off for me and placed it behind my seat when we arrived and when we exited he made sure to help me get my jacket back on. He paid for everything and took initiative whenever needed. He was exactly like his brother in every way except their personalities were so different. One was reserved, laid back, chill while the other was forward, open, and animated.

Right around one in the afternoon we were casually strolling around the city.

"I need a blunt." Snoop interrupted our conversation.

"Back to the crib?"

"Nah, my apartment literally five minutes from here. We

can chill over there," he suggested. I agreed it was a good idea to just hit his place instead of driving that long ass distance back to the house.

Snoops apartment was a well decorated bachelor's pad. Large studio apartment with a steel stairwell right next to the entrance that led up to the bedroom on a balcony overlooking the rest of the apartment. The first floor included his kitchen, small dining room, living space. and a large spa bathroom in the furthest corner.

"This is a pretty nice place for you." I spoke as he moved around upstairs.

"For me? What's that supposed to mean?" he asked, peeking his head over the balcony.

"It means that I expected you to live like a typical single male. Not like a middle aged man that owns a law firm or something," I elaborated.

"That's fucked up. So basically you're saying you didn't think I had taste. How rude, Pinky," he joked with me.

"It's not that," I spoke out loud as I made myself comfortable on his suede navy couch.

"Yea, yea," he blew me off coming back down the stairs to join me on the couch. He brought with him a double barrel bong filled partially with water. Snoop added the bud to the pipe and sparked his bong.

"You comfortable or what?" He looked over at me curled up on the corner of his couch.

"Don't be funny." I ignored him.

"So do I get a chance to ask you shit? I mean since I finally got you talking to me," he over exaggerated.

"Shoot." I entertained him.

"I always wanted to know what size titties you have," he

seriously asked as he hit the bong.

"Really? That's the pressing question you had to ask." I was annoyed.

"Nah for real tho. I been wondering that forever. Whatever size they are. That's my favorite size," he laughed.

I mugged him then I answered, "34F."

He nodded his head. "I'll have to remember that when I'm filling out my wants on singlepeoplemeet.com." We both laughed.

"A more serious question tho. What you gon tell King when he asks you what you did today?" Good question. What was I gonna tell him?

"I haven't thought about it honestly." I kept it real.

"Well we need to talk about this so our stories sync up. You know." He was right.

"I could just tell him I kicked it with you."

He laughed. "That's up to you."

"What would you do?" I genuinely wanted to know.

"Well…" he paused. "Tell him the truth. That way he'll become suspicious and keep you away from me."

"And if I lie?"

"You'll get to see me more. But I can't promise I'll keep my hands to myself. The choice is yours, Pinky." He ended the conversation and went back to his solo session.

I ended up falling asleep on the couch. Travis was up banging music through his headphones when I woke up. He was cleaning up, doing laundry, and smoking weed all while I slept. I never meet a person that smoked so much weed. I don't think I've ever seen him sober.

"Bout time you got up, sleepy head ass," he clowned me.

I mugged him then I got up and stretched.

"We gotta go. I need to make a play." He signaled me to get ready. I got up, put my boots on, and pulled my hair into a ponytail.

"Where we going?" I asked him as we walked out the door.

"Not far. Twenty minutes from here. I'm picking up a drop then need to make the deposit," he said, unlocking the door to his Range and getting in.

"We might as well run the drags back since we out this way." The drags are the money bags we give the street distributors. I rode with Loc once to run drags and noticed the same bags in the back of Snoop's whip.

"Nah, I don't run drags. My little niggas do all that shit for me in the morning. Only reason I run all the drops is because King don't trust nobody else's name on the bank account as a trustee other than me." His statement made sense to me. I nodded. Snoop turned up his music. I watched him transform from his mellow attitude to a Street Dealer. Snoop was attractive and he knew it. His hair was always cut, lips were never chapped, and he always smelled good. Plus, his body type was athletic, you could tell he went to the gym often.

"It's your turn to start our conversation," he demanded. He glanced over at me then he changed his attention back to the road.

"Ummm," I hesitated. "Who you dating?" I smiled after I asked.

He laughed, genuinely. "Ummm," he hesitated. "I date this one girl. This slim cool chick that I fuck around with tough. Shorty tryna get me to wife her but I ain't really with all that."

His response sparked my interest. "You not feeling her or something?"

"She alright." He attempted to be vague. "She cute and she cool; I just ain't really into her like that," he answered honestly.

"Why not?"

"Because she trip about me smoking so much weed," he laughed. "I know that shit sound petty but ain't no way I'm about to stop smoking weed for a female. Well, for you I would but not anyone else." He snuck that one in.

I laughed. "I wouldn't tell you to stop smoking weed. I wouldn't tell a grown person ever to do something particular with their life because I wouldn't want that shit to come my way either."

"See this why I fuck with you." He nodded his head. "How old are you? You been dancing at Mike's for a minute now but you don't look that old."

"I'm twenty-two. I been at Mike's for about four years now."

"Damn you was a baby back then, Pinky. Why you been in the club so long?"

"I had to. I didn't have any other career offers and I needed to make real money in order to take care of myself."

"I feel you. I'm twenty-two, too. But, I just started making real money like two years ago with King. King put all of us on. My ass wasn't on shit before bro started grindin tough."

"You really been going to Mike's since you were 16?" I asked him.

"On my mama. I think I remember when you first started. You always been fine but you got badder over time," he elaborated. I smiled.

"We both grew up in Mike's. That's funny," I added to the conversation.

"I was all over this city back then. Acting up." We pulled up to the spot where the exchange would take place.

"I'll be back." Snoop grabbed his pistol out the center console and tucked it as he got out the car. I pulled down the glove-compartment just to make sure there was an extra strap in there for backup. There was. I watched our surroundings. Snoop was back in two minutes. We pulled off and drove the eight miles to meet the Brink's truck to make the drop. After that, Snoop dropped me off back at the crib.

"So what's it going to be like between me and you from here on out?" Snoop asked as he pulled into the driveway.

"What you mean? It's gonna be chill between us. That's really the only option we have at this point." He nodded in agreement.

"I'll see you around, shorty." He spoke to me, then I got out and he drove off.

The house was still. Aaron still wasn't back home yet. I immediately felt like I was missing something after separating from Travis. I enjoyed the attention and the conversation.

11

Round Table

It's impossible to know who you'll encounter next on your journey. Sometimes it's individuals who you would have preferred not to meet and other times it's people who you never want to see go.

This morning started off hectic. Instead of waking up at six in the morning in bed by myself, I woke up to an empty bed and a packed living room. King, Loc, and four of their distributors sat in our living room discussing business. I snuck into the kitchen to start breakfast. I had a house full of men very early in the morning, it was only a matter of time before they were hungry. I warmed up two pans on the stove to cook a few packs of bacon, started brewing a pot of coffee, and whipped up some buttermilk pancake batter from scratch. Our kitchen is a pretty nice size with a large island, new stainless steel appliances, and black marble floors. But, what I loved most is that it is a very open space yet it's only visible point from the living room is through the open space for the bar. I could easily hide in the kitchen and still see all the activity when I wanted. Snoop barged in through the backdoor right into the kitchen just as I was taking the bacon from the skillet.

"I see I'm right on time" he said to me as a greeting. I just looked up at him, not saying a word. I could tell he was far from on time. King had been holding a meeting for the last forty-five minutes and here he comes just now walking in the door.

"Good morning," I spoke. He smiled at me then rushed into the living room to join the others. King mugged him as he took a seat on the couch then he continued with his agenda.

I eavesdropped on their entire conversation. According to King, sales have been down over the last two months ever since they took that unexpected hiatus. Loc and the other distributors presented plans for improvement and King shot down every idea. He said that those ideas were either too risky or not risky enough. Then, Snoop finally spoke.

"Why don't we just capitalize off the small vendors? Up the price by five percent just to get sales back steady until our more high profile customers have more requests. Busy season is only a few months away; we just need to maintain until then," he stated then he went back to smoking his blunt.

His points were valid. So valid that no one, not even King, pushed back.

"That's actually a good idea. I'll need you to draft that operational plan and we can put it into play," King followed.

"No can do, Boss. I don't do paperwork. Not really my strong point if you catch my drift." Snoop added filling his lungs with smoke.

"Time for you to pick up some additional skills. I'll need that plan formalized by end of week." King put his foot down and concluded his meeting then everyone grabbed breakfast.

Once everyone left, Aaron met me in the kitchen. He wrapped his arms around my waist from the back and rested his head on my shoulder. I embraced his gesture.

"I miss you. I never get a chance to kick it with you anymore. The operation been too unstable," he opened up to me.

"I've noticed. I've been trying to stay out of your hair. One less thing to worry about," I reassured him.

"I'd much rather worry about you." He kissed my face then he released his embrace. "I'll be in my office but sometime soon I'll schedule a getaway for us," he said then he disappeared.

Later that night, I was scheduled to work a ten hour shift at Mike's. I came in at five and don't get off until three. It was Thirsty Thursday so all the drinks were half off. On nights like this a lot of females come to the club which attracts more men. I had a performance every hour of my shift with a two song minimum per usual. I was beyond ready to get off. Tonight I just wasn't feeling it. I did my normal stage routine, collected my money then tried to hide for the rest of the night. I ducked off in the corner of the club closest to the bar and talked to Draya all night.

"Girl I'm sick of this place" she vented.

"Really? You just now coming to that conclusion," I responded.

"After Mike cheap ass tried to take half of my tips the other night because the cash register came up short. He got me fucked up," she added. I laughed.

"You know these lil yamps in here stay stealing from

him."

"Yea but that's them. That ain't got shit to do with my pockets." Draya was pissed.

"You know I feel you." I reassured her trying to keep the conversation going when I noticed her attention change. Just at that moment Snoop walked up. He was fitted in black slim fit slacks, dark olive green button down, and all black Nike boots. He took a seat right next to me.

"What can I get for you, Snoop?" Draya leaned over the counter to give him extra close flirtatious attention. But, in her defense, she's like that with all her customers.

"D'ussé on the rocks."

"That'll be ten, baby."

"Here's something for you, too." He flirted back handing her a twenty. I rolled my eyes at their exchange.

"Really?" I attempted to get his attention.

He turned his attention to me pretending as if he didn't know I was sitting here. "Oh what's up, Ms. Pink Dolla.".

"Don't be funny, Travis."

"I didn't know you were working tonight." Draya placed his drink on the bar then walked away.

"Yea sure," I commented. He smiled at my envious behavior.

"What you doin here anyway? Don't you have an operation plan to complete?" I brought up his assignment from King earlier.

He shook his head as he sipped his drink. "I'm not doin that shit."

"Why not? I thought your plan was good."

"I do too. But I ain't really with all that formal documentation bullshit. That's the shit King do. I'm just a street nigga."

"Sounds like you're downplaying yourself." I refuted his point.

"Just like you do every time I tell you fine ass fuck." He glanced over at me to see my reaction. I didn't react. "Why you not out there making money anyway?" He changed the subject.

I shook my head. "I'm not in the mood to deal with these thirsty ass niggas today."

"I feel you. They do be thirsty off yo lil thick ass." He glanced over my thighs and my hips.

"Exactly and I'm not in the mood for it. I'll stick to my stage performances tonight." Then I pulled my phone out of my thigh high boots to check the time. "Speaking of, I'm up next." I got up and headed to the stage. He watched me walk away then he proceeded to enjoy his drink. I performed for my two song minimum and watched Snoop's reactions. He didn't move from his spot until I was done. He paid careful attention. After I got off the stage he got up and moved around.

• • •

Later that night while driving home "Lifetime" by Erykah Badu played on a local radio station. It was all too eerie. Here I was driving in a brand new BMW that King bought for me without me even asking yet and I was thinking about Snoop the entire way home. He had completely taken over my subconscious. I day-dreamed about him, wondered what he was doing when he wasn't around, and when I did see him I was excited to be in his presence. A man that I could barely stand to talk to a few months back evolved into somebody I was interested in. This can't be real. Then, I snapped back into reality. I was dating King and that was that.

Upon pulling up to our mini mansion I noticed that all the cars that were scattered around the outside of the house this morning were gone. I pulled into the driveway, opened the garage, and noticed the Audi was parked. Aaron was home. I pulled beside his car, gathered my work bag from the trunk, and went inside. Before closing the door I let the garage down. I carefully maneuvered through the breezeway that led directly into the kitchen. There were no lights on, no TV. Just soft subtle music playing in the background. I placed my bag on the floor in a corner. As I made my way into the living room I noticed candles. Lots of candles. All four corner tables, the center table, and the fireplace was covered in aromatherapy candles. The scent was soothing, soft, and relaxing. Aaron came down the stairs, shirtless with just his slacks on. I loved it when he walked around with his shirt off because he rarely did. He was so fit, chiseled chest covered in tattoos, firm arms, and flawless skin. He approached me, opening his arms to invite me near him. He lured me in and we embraced. He didn't say much to me other than "I missed you." He simply led with action and created a completely stress free environment. He lightly lifted me into his arms; with my legs straddling his waist, he held my body and softly kissed my neck as he walked over to the couch. He sat down leaving me in his lap facing him. He grabbed a glass of champagne from the table behind the couch and handed it to me then he grabbed the second one for himself.

"I just wanted to show you how much I appreciate you." We toasted to his words.

He finished his glass and placed the empty flute back on

the table then he took my half full glass and did the same. He continued to massage my neck with his soft firm lips. He knew exactly which spots to kiss to make me react. I pulled my shirt over my head and threw it across the room. My black lace push up bra held my supple titties high on my chest, distracting him. King gently picked me up and laid me lengthwise against the large couch. He unbuttoned then slid off my jeans revealing my matching lace thong panties. He kissed my body from head to toe with passion. His hands roamed slowly across my skin as he resisted licking me. Once he couldn't resist any more he popped the front hook on my bra and licked my firm nipples vigorously. I moaned. My panties were soaking. He was zoned in on my body. His hands moved firmly with purpose and his tongue stroked my piercings leaving his saliva all over my titties. He stood up then pulled his pants and his Polo boxers off exposing his manhood. He was solid hard. He threw his leg over my body and straddled my chest. He tapped my nipples with the tip of his dick then he pressed his hard shaft between my titties. He palmed my F's in each of his hands then he thrusted between my slippery breast. He gripped firmly adding as much pressure between my titties and his shaft. He held his head back and enjoyed every single stroke. Once he lost his grip he slid, effortlessly, into my mouth and fucked my throat. I held my lips firm adding resistance.

His mouth hung open like he wanted to moan but he held in his passion. He pulled out and held his meat in his left hand. He stood up. With his right hand he slid my soaking wet panties off and threw them across the room. Again, he tapped the head of his dick against my clit then he slid his length inside me. I gasped. He filled me up. He pulled me up onto his lap and bounced me on his dick. He placed his hands on my ass, gripping all my fat and he buried his head between my titties. He wouldn't let me take control. He pulled me up and down on his shaft over and over again making me scream his name. I climaxed all over his dick. He licked his lips as he watched me cum. He pulled himself out and kissed my face then he flipped me over the couch with my ass up. His dick was covered in a clear creamy sauce. He again tapped his dick against my cheeks then he slid right back in. I yelled his name and every curse word I could think of. He stroked me deep. My ass bounced against his abs with every thrust. He fucked me harder and harder, rubbing my clit with every last stroke. This time when I busted I called him Daddy. Daddy fucked me good. A few strokes after I came he pulled out and covered my entire ass with white syrup. His body glistened with sweat.

After he caught his breath, we went upstairs and showered together.

"You always make it worth the wait," I told him while we bathed.

"I feel the same way about you." I smiled.

Once we finished showering, Aaron put on some boxers and immediately laid down. I did the same after I threw on one of his shirts. My body was still tingling from our sex so I stayed up for a few minutes but Aaron was knocked out as soon as his head hit the pillows. Before we went to sleep that night, I checked my messages:

Snoop: I wish you were here.

12

Layers

You'd be surprised what you could learn about someone if you took the time.

A month had passed by without me hearing a single word from my pops. In retrospect, that didn't seem like a long time seeing that I went years without speaking to my family at one point. But this time it was different. I knew he was in trouble. I knew he was somewhere suffering and in need. Though I did want to help him, I just couldn't bring myself to feel sympathy for him. I kept thinking about all the times he left me stuck out. I thought about those homeless nights when I slept in stolen cars or on train station benches. I remembered how I wished he would come find me, take me back home, and help me put my life back together. He never came. No one ever came.

I was following up on a lead that Nino gave me on a Benz that's been parked in an alleyway downtown for a few days now. That was literally the nature of Nino and I's relationship, he only called when there was money to be made. I usually found my own merchandise, executed the pickup, then dropped it off at the pawn shop. But, this time

Nino had his eye on a fairly new CLK Benz. I told him I would check it out.

I took the D bus out to downtown from the outskirts. I didn't drive my car just in case this was a good lead and I needed to quickly pick up the merchandise. The car was parked on the corner on the far end of downtown. I scoped out the scene before I scoped out the car. It's a groggy day so there wasn't much activity happening on the block. I did notice that the car wasn't near any immediate businesses or apartment buildings. Across the street from where the car was parked was an unkempt empty parking lot. I walked a little closer to the car but kept a fair distance. I pulled out my binoculars and took a detailed look inside the car. Leather seats, woodgrain dash, and no cosmetic issues. It was obvious this was a brand new car.

I also took a look at the locks and saw that the doors were completely unlocked, all four of them. At that moment I knew this was a bait car. Though I watch very little TV, I do read the newspaper daily. And for the last couple of months NYPD has been trying to cut their losses related to the car jackings. The car showed all the signs; a brand new car on the lower income side of downtown sitting out in broad daylight with no tint on the windows so anyone passing could easily peer inside, and to top it off the doors were unlocked. That was a good try by them, a very enticing catch, but I ain't going for it. I immediately became uninterested and headed out.

"Yo, Ally, tell me you got good news," Nino answered my call.

"No can do. That joint was a setup. I wouldn't touch that whip with a ten foot pole unless I'm tryna see twenty years in the pen."

"Man damn! You sure?"

"Absolutely positive. But, if you wanna try it out feel free but I ain't doin it."

"Nah, I trust yo judgement. That's exactly why I hit yo line. Good looking out."

"Yea no problem." We concluded our conversation.

I spent the rest of my day prowling through the streets trying to catch somebody slipping. Jacking cars was nothing like the steady cash flow of stripping. I put in hard hours some days and come up with nothing. But, in the strip club, I can barely shake my ass and still walk out of there with a stack. Nonetheless, I kept my side hustle because on those days that I hit big it was well worth the wait. I had stacked over eighty thousand dollars from dropping off cars at the pawn shop. And I'm saving every penny, just in case I get that call from my pops. Aaron was making it easy as hell for me to save. He takes care of all the bills, paid for my car in cash, feeds me daily, and gives me a daily stipend every morning. I haven't spent one dollar of my own money since I moved in with him. I think he's doing that because he wants to show me that it's ok to stop stripping and that all my needs would be taken care of. But what he didn't understand was that I'm not stripping to survive anymore. I strip and work at the pawn shop to stack my cash flow for a larger matter. A situation that I'm not sure is even going to happen but the last thing I would want is to be unprepared. Plus, if I stopped working what would I be? A stay at home girlfriend?

The streets stayed dry all day. I was roaming through an area that had been hit a few times by some of our competitors. I saw the news stories. My theory is people are finally getting some common sense and locking their shit up tight. I sent Nino a text:

Me: Streets dry. Ain't no moves shakin. I'm clockin out.

Nino: Fasho

Nino wasn't hurting for shit. He had plenty of weight coming into the pawn shop on a daily basis. He also knew that some days were dry and he preferred that the street crew was smart about their actions rather than take the chance of having the Feds get involved. Also, the nature of our relationship was a lot different. Nino treated me more like family instead of an employee. When he put me on he did it because I told him that I was in a bind and not the other way around. Once I got on my feet he asked me to stay connected with the shop. He said he liked having a soft body around instead of all the dudes that do runs for him. I agreed, but I told him I make my own schedule and not to sweat me about shit. He was cool with it.

I made it all the way back to the house to chill. I was scheduled off from the club so I planned on relaxing. I really didn't like being off but I was getting a little restless from working so much so I decided to appreciate some me time.

When I got home my BMW was still parked out in front, Aaron's Audi was still missing from the garage but Loc's truck was parked in the middle of the driveway. I didn't remember there being an operation meeting scheduled for today but they also don't tell me everything. When I walked inside through the side door into the kitchen Loc and Snoop were both standing in the kitchen taking shots of Cognac. They both changed their direction to me and immediately ceased their conversation. I remembered that he texted me a few nights back and that I never responded. I avoided that conversation completely.

"See that makes me think y'all were talking about me," I opened up the conversation.

"Yea we were," Snoop answered glaring at me as I passed by them. Loc didn't correct him but I assumed he was joking.

"Un huh I'ma need both you to get some business."

"Technically you are our business, Pinky," Loc broke his silence.

"Yea, speaking of, where were you all day?" Loc asked.

"Um minding my business. Is that okay with you?" I asked, walking into the living room. They followed behind me.

"Depends on what kind of activities are included in 'minding your business'."

"Really, Snoop? Why are you grilling me like this?"

"If you weren't doing nothing then it's not grilling," Snoop added

"We just gotta keep an eye on you, Pinky. These streets not safe," Loc followed up.

I sat down on the couch, Snoop sat right next to me and Loc sat on the loveseat facing the TV.

"I grew up in these streets. I don't need nobody to keep an eye on me."

They dropped the subject.

The sun was starting to set, filling the entire house with light. I took full advantage of the setting while I painted in my studio. When I painted I became another person; someone who didn't have to hustle daily, a person that was perfectly content with painting on her easel from sun up to sun down.

"What's it like?" Travis asked.

"What's what like?" I was confused.

"You know, having this layer of depth that most people don't know exist about you," he said as he watched me paint. He casually walked around my studio looking at my latest work then, he made himself comfortable on one of the plush benches in the middle of the room.

"I don't know. I never thought about it." I was honest.

"I just assume it's hard for you because I'm sure most of them thirsty niggas don't ask you about your dreams, goals, or talents."

"Some of em do. I don't tell em though. I know they don't really care; they're just tryna come off as different than your average nigga."

"I care."

I looked up from my easel to look at him. He was facing the bay window gazing out at the night sky. "I can tell," I replied.

The nature of me and Travis' relationship started to evolve subtly. We casually spent more and more time together. Our time together was unintentional but receptive and inviting. It was almost like we were dating on accident. He was at our house way more than Aaron and most days Aaron would instruct either him or Loc to keep an eye on me. Travis took his assignment literal; making sure he was in my immediate presence anytime we were at the same location. He also spent a lot of time at Mike's, even when I wasn't working.

On days that I did work he always sat hidden in a corner or in a private VIP section but he kept his eyes on me. According to the bartenders, Snoop was way more social on the nights I didn't work. But when I was there I barely even saw him talk to anyone let alone get lap dances. It was almost like he was on his best behavior when I was around. I started getting into the habit of looking for him every time I hit the stage. I always made my shows good but when he was there I was trying to impress him. I'm pretty sure he noticed.

"What's the backstory with you and King?" I asked attempting to break our silence.

"That's just my older brother. You know, same ol story. You don't have older siblings?"

I rolled my eyes. "I do. An older sister that I never got along with. Which seems different than what you and King have."

"Ah yea that's my boy. He only a few years older than me so we been tight since the beginning. Growing up I thought that nigga was the coolest nigga on the planet. He was my brother and my pops at the same time. Our father was murdered when we were younger. King held it down for me and moms even though he was barely twelve at the time."

"Damn. That's mad respectful."

"Yea dude is a beast. But don't get it twisted we had many fights and arguments over the years. Son pulled the heat out on my ass many times."

"Why?"

He shook his head. "I'm the younger more hard-headed sibling. Do you really have to ask that?"

"I guess it's different for me. I'm the youngest but I'm the level headed one. My sister is an ain't shit ass lazy broke ass bitch. Her neglect forced me to be more independent and serious. She ain't never took care of me or her own kids for that matter."

"Damn, how many kids she got?"

"Two boys. Two different daddy's. She live with my mama in BK and she damn near thirty."

"Yea that's pitiful. What about yo folks tho?"

"They separated when we were in grade school cause my pops has a bad ass gambling addiction. He put my mom through hell for decades until she finally put him out. I barely saw him and because my mama had to work eighteen hour days just to keep our house, I barely saw her. My sister was a tramp ass slut bringing grown ass men to our house when she was barely fifteen. I remember one day one of them sleazy ass mothafuckas tried to come in my room."

His face grew worried. "What did you?!"

"I pulled out a knife I kept hidden under my bed and stabbed his ass. Otherwise he woulda tried me. I was nine. My sister didn't do shit. Dude left drippin blood before I could even call the police."

"Fuck. That's mad wild. So when did shit get good for you? I mean because you seem put together now."

"Mike's. That club saved me believe it or not. Without that place I wouldn't have ate or had a place to stay. I left my mom's house when I was sixteen. Never finished high school. I slept on the streets for years. When I turned eighteen, Mike gave me my first legit job. I owe him more than I could ever repay."

He looked at me in a way I've ever seen from him before. His eyes were filled with compassion. But you could tell he didn't feel sorry for me.

"The more and more I talk to you the more beautiful you get. Other than being hard to get to, you just an all-around bad ass woman."

I blushed.

"I know my brother loves you but I don't think he sees you the same way I do.

"What do you mean?" I was curious.

"There's so many dimensions to you. That first layer is just a front, a wall, that you use to weed out bullshit people. The second layer is this goal oriented, driven, cool ass person. Which is the layer I think King fucks with the most just because he the same way. Then there's this third layer, the gentle, observant, curious, abstract you. That's the layer that makes you paint early in the morning or in the middle of the night. The same layer that allows you to freely open up and embrace life. That's the layer I like."

I digested his thoughts. "I thought you liked my stripper layer though?"

He laughed. "Hell yeah that too. Everybody likes that

layer."

I laughed too and continued with my painting.

He stood up and made his way to the door. "I just wish I met you first," he said right before he left the room.

Later that night, Snoop slept on the couch while Loc made his final runs. The lights in house were always blaring at about two in the morning because that was the time King usually made it back home and the time I got off work. King came into the house, dropped his bag by the door, and immediately wrapped his arms around me. He embraced me with love, kissed my forehead, and then let me go.

"Ay get yo sleepy ass up," King yelled at Snoop, throwing a pillow at his head.

"Son chill out with all that shit." Snoop stood up and stretched his long body. "What the fuck happened with Chino and them?" Snoop asked.

I didn't know very much about Chino but I did know that he was some type of counterpart that the boys always worked with. He lived in Toronto and that's who King went to go visit this morning.

"Once Loc pulls up I'll fill you in," King answered, pulling out the D'ussé bottle and setting it at the round table with a few shot glasses. I stood in the kitchen and watched them move around. King and Snoop behaved like twins almost. It was like they could tell what the other one was thinking. Snoop opened the fridge then King handed him a glass. Snoop filled the glass with ice then handed it back to King. King poured water into the glass then handed the leftover water and water bottle to Snoop. Snoop killed the leftover water and threw away the bottle. King drank the cold water from the glass filled with ice. They did all of this without saying a word to each other. When Loc pulled up they both looked toward the window to make sure it was him. King looked out the peephole at the front door and Snoop looked out the window through the sheer drapes. Then, they both nodded in confirmation that it was indeed Loc in the driveway. Snoop sat at his usual seat at the round table and started breaking down buds into little white papers. Loc came inside and sat down at the table opposite from Snoop.

"You too, Ally." King motioned me over as he took his seat at the head of the table. Snoop and Loc both looked at him funny then Snoop gave me look; one of those looks where he was checking me out to make sure I measured up. I wasn't intimidated. This would be my very first round table. Sure I had heard many of their round table discussions but this was the first time I actually got a seat at the table.

"So what you got for us, boss?" Loc asked attentively. Snoop lit his joint and reared back in his chair and I sat there with my hands folded in my lap.

"I talked to Chino today. He offered me a business proposition," he started.

"What? He tryna push some of our work or what?" Snoop asked with his lungs full of smoke.

"Not quite. He wants to take the chop shop off our hands in exchange for some of his territory up in Canada."

"The fuck he want the chop shop for?"

"He really wants the chop shop and our entire Runner portfolio," King explained.

I had no idea what the chop shop or the Runner portfolio was but what I did know was that Snoop didn't like this business proposition.

"Man fuck no! The Runners is my shit. Always been my shit." Snoop stood up.

"Man sit yo ass down," King calmly instructed. "Need I remind you the Runners is *our* shit! Ever since I pulled yo ass outta that jam a few years back. And the fact that I manage that shit more than yo ass ever has, you lucky I'm even asking yo long ass for your opinion." Snoop sat back down.

"How much territory we talking?" Loc asked a strategic question.

"The entire Southwest side of Toronto. It's a big ass territory and there's already established clientele."

"I think it's a fair trade," Loc added.

"Fair? How?" Snoop was salty.

"Dog, the Runners ain't been nothing but trouble lately. It's way too hard to get our money outta them fools and we really had to pick up too many bodies over that shit."

"Loc is right. It's been mostly a liability for us and the way yo wild ass is set up I can't take a chance with you getting caught." King pointed at Snoop. Snoop didn't say nothing.

"Have we thought about why this Chino cat is so willing to give up his territory?" I finally spoke. All three of them turned to me as if they even forgot I was sitting there.

"Yea, have we thought about that?" Snoop broke the silence.

"He didn't go into the details of all that; he just said he was looking to get into something different."

"I say we go check it out. Scope the area and make sure this ain't a setup," I followed up.

Everybody nodded in agreement.

"That's a solid suggestion. We'll add that to the action plan," King nodded.

It appeared that I added some balance to the round table. You had King who was obviously the Type A dictator style leader, Loc who was Type B and way too easy going, and then Snoop who was always extremely far left. I added a voice of reason, a different far right perspective.

"On to the next order of business, let's talk about the pawn shop, Ally."

My mouth dropped. Snoop and Loc both looked at me with their eyebrows raised.

"That's where you be at in the middle of the day, Pinky?" Loc was surprised.

"You boasting cars too?! Damn what can't you do?" Snoop was even more surprised than Loc.

"I talked to my boy Nino on the way back from Toronto and he casually bragged about one his boosters. After he described you, I put two and two together. You can't keep doing that shit, that's too much heat." King gave me my first demand.

"I'm fucking good at boosting cars. Probably the best in this city," I bragged.

"I don't care. You gotta get out of it. We need at least one person in the group with clean hands. We can't all be crooks," King spoke.

He was right. That wasn't smart for all of us to be dirty. What would happen if we got caught up? Who bails us out?

"Alright fine. I'll stop jacking cars." I rolled my eyes.

Snoop busted out laughing. "Either I'm really high or this shit is funny as fuck. You like a supervillain. Super Stripping

Carjacking Woman!" He laughed with tears in his eyes. Then, King and Loc started laughing which made me laugh too.

13

Family Therapy

Address your issues before they address you.

This particular morning my internal calendar went off reminding me it was a few days after the first of the month. That meant I needed make moves to BK to get Mom her mortgage payment. It was early; well before the sun even thought about waking up. King was already out making his moves. The house was silent. I now preferred the mellow feeling that early morning gives off so I left the house silent and dim while I got myself together. I took my time getting ready. I enjoyed my steamy hot shower; waking up my body as I cleared my mind. I knew I needed to get very close to my inner peace before I went to deal with my family. I allowed the steam to open my pores and free my skin from any built up toxins, I bathed with all natural soaps to restore and replenish, and I allowed the warm water to run through my hair as I stood in our large shower with my eyes closed.

After I was fully dressed I dropped a few rolled stacks into my backpack, grabbed my phone, keys, and wallet. Then, I pulled my compact 9mm from the nightstand drawer. I checked the clip and counted my rounds, flipped the safety, and placed it in my bag as well. I slid my feet in my navy Timbs and headed through the house toward the front door. The sun was barely peeking through the window and the house was still silent. I made sure there were no drops, notes, or unfinished work sitting around the house before I exited through the garage. I got inside my Z5 and flipped the garage opener. The interior in my car was peanut butter leather, full wood grain panels with steel accents. I drove the kind of car that I would have anxiously looked to steal and drop off at the pawn shop. That's the reason why I made sure to keep it locked up.

An hour later I pulled up in front of my mom's crib. Nobody was outside. The house looked exactly how it did last time I was here; screen door tattered and ragged, the lawn was unkempt, and the windows needed a serious power wash. The dope fiends were gathered at the corner of the street as usual. I put my car in park, threw my bag over my shoulder, and stepped toward the front porch. I checked to make sure the door was locked before I knocked. I knocked three times then I waited. I knocked a fourth and fifth time but with a lot more force. The door started to creak open as someone took their time letting me in. It was my mama. She stood behind the door looking more frail than ever before. She was always thin but her thinness this time looked more like weakness.

"Oh, Ally!" she was happy to see me. "Come on in baby girl." She pushed the screen door back and stepped to the side.

"Hey, Mama," I spoke as I hugged her. I was just happy to see her standing this time as opposed to laying in the bed.

"That's a nice car you got there." She pointed out

my BMW. "That dancing club sure is treating you well."

"Yeah something like that." I neglected to mention Aaron.

"Bring yaself on in here. I just started prepping for brunch today. You know my book club meeting is every first Sunday and I'm hosting today," she explained as I followed her into the kitchen.

"I completely forgot about those meetings. You been doing that for years now."

"Eleven years this summer, child. We going strong. I gotta have something to keep me happy around here. Especially since you don't come see me nothing but once a month." She glared at me from the stove as she stirred her collard greens.

"It ain't even like that. I live far from here and I work a lot."

"Or is it just because you and Jade just can't seem to get along?"

"Can we keep the Jade conversations to a minimum? I'm having a good morning so far and I want to keep it that way."

"You know she here. Sleeping still. As usual."

"Where's Duke and Cameron?" I asked.

"Well," she paused. "Duke is in his room sleeping. But, Cameron's father and his legal representation came over here about three weeks ago and handed Jade a full custody order from a federal judge. I've told her plenty of times that she has to go to custody court but she never listened. Now I don't have no clue when we gone get Baby Cam back."

"She doesn't have any custody rights?" I was shocked.

"Nope. Can't even see the boy one day out the year

because she missed every last court date."

I shook my head. "I bet she don't even care."

"She cared that first day but ever since then she ain't even attempted to call the man just to go over and visit the baby. I been taking the bus with Duke over there on Friday's to go see him but she don't come with us."

"She's a sad ass individual."

"Now don't be like that. Jade had it hard growing up."

"Really, Mama? Jade had it hard? Are you serious?"

"Well, she had to watch me and ya daddy go through that whole divorce. I think that really affected how she feels about relationships."

"Oh and I guess I was just invisible at the time. I saw all the same shit Jade saw plus more, at a younger age at that. Jade fat ass don't get no excuses with me. You and Daddy gave her every option in the book to go to college and do something with her life but what did she decide to do? Hoe around."

"You say that like I wouldn't have gave you them same options."

"I didn't even get that far in life. I was truant every single year of high school. Hell, I dropped out a whole year before you even found out. I don't want no sympathy from you or anyone else but please know the difference between me and yo other lazy ass daughter."

Just as I was finishing that statement, Jade popped her head into the kitchen. She was in her draws and an overnight t-shirt. Her hair was all over her head. Seconds after she popped up a big burly man walked up wearing just his basketball shorts with his gut hanging out.

"I knew I heard somebody in here nagging," Jade

spoke.

"Man who the fuck is this sloppy ass nigga? Put a fucking shirt on! You in my mama house, boy show some respect."

"Ally calm down." My mama walked over and put her hand on my shoulder.

"Jade who is this?" I calmed my voice.

"This my man. If yo bougie ass came around more you would have known that."

"I was here last month and you wasn't with no nigga. Matter of fact, you was still getting fucked by Duke's daddy. Why the fuck you got this big ass mothafucka over here? He doesn't have his own crib?"

"Nah we can't kick it at my crib." the man spoke.

"And yo ass can't kick it here either. This my mama house you not welcome here. Get yo shit and get out!" I demanded.

My mama took a seat at the table because she knew this was about to get real.

"He ain't gotta go nowhere! This is Mama house. She pays the bills so he can stay," Jade opened her trap.

"Well, actually I pay the bills in this bitch!" I opened up my backpack and threw the stacks on the table.

"So like I said, get yo shit and get out!"

Jade looked over at my mama who had her head buried in her hands at this point.

"Mama, Ally pays all the bills?" My mama nodded. "Why you didn't tell me that? I don't need no handouts from this bitch!"

"Oh you don't? Is that right? So, Jade exactly how you gon afford a twenty-three hundred dollar mortgage payment plus all the utilities? Cause that lil job you got at the beauty supply ain't gon cut it and apparently you not making enough money selling yo worn out pussy."

Jade swung at me, landing a right punch against my cheek. I immediately stepped back to get some space between us then I threw a combo right back at her ass. Mama started screaming at us to stop fighting but I kept throwing blows. Jade ended up folding, trying to protect her face while I worked her big ass. After a while, her guy friend jumps in and puts his arm around my neck. He started to apply pressure but before the hold got too tight I pulled my head through his arms, freeing myself and immediately grabbed my gun out my open bag that was sitting on the table. I pointed the gun dead at dude's face.

"Don't you ever put yo fucking hands on me," I said in a low but firm voice.

Mama screamed out in tears full of pain. Jade got her big ass up off the floor and her male friend stood there with his hands up.

"Now I'ma say this one more time. Get yo shit and get the fuck out." I lowered the gun, reassuring everyone that I wasn't planning on killing anyone. Dude walked off, grabbed his shirt, then walked out the front door. Jade followed behind him.

I looked at my mom. "If you want me to keep paying for this house don't let no more random ass men sleep in here. You think it's harmless but you don't know these people's intentions. And if nobody in this house wants to see the issue with my nephew meeting a new ain't shit ass nigga every month then I guess I'll just have to be the one to say it. Be a better grandmother to him than you were a mom to me." I placed my gun back in my bag and walked out the front door.

Jade stood at the edge of the front lawn crying like she lost her husband or something.

"Look what you did?!" She screamed at me. I just looked at her sad ass. "That was a good man and you ran him off!"

"You know what Jade? Have you stopped to think about why that man didn't want you at his house? Did you even think about how easy it was for him to put his arm around my neck? You think I fucked something up for you? Bitch, I'm saving you. Just like I always had to. I always had to save you from niggas that could care less about yo ass! Where were you when these 'good men' were trying to put their hands on me?! No fucking where but I stay saving yo ass every chance I get.

Did you cry this much when they came and took yo son away? Do you get mad at yourself for not being able to take care of Duke? That's the shit you should be worried about. And to think you and Mama always wondering why I don't come around here. All of you remind me of my childhood, those gloomy ass days where all we saw were drug addicts, fights, and no good men taking advantage of women. I don't want that for myself. And at the time when I left here originally, I thought I was running away from my home but really I was getting away from all the negative bullshit that this family brings. It took six years for me to realize that what I did for myself was the best decision ever. And guess what? I'm happy now, something you'll never be."

I walked away. I didn't want to hear her side of the story. She hadn't even fully formulated her views anyway.

Jade had been masking her pain for years. So much that she doesn't even know why she behaved the way she did. She never left her environment to understand why where she is and what she does is so toxic. She never grew up. She's still that twelve year old girl sneaking men into her parent's house.

Today, for the first time ever, I felt bad for Jade. Watching her cry over a man that I could tell didn't have any feelings for her was so sad. Today, for the first time ever, I prayed for Jade. I asked the most high to free her spirit from the pain that holds her back so that she could be free.

14

A Full Clip

Stay ready.

"I can't miss the shipment today. It's a big ass move and Chino wanna meet today," King explained.

"Man I ain't going to meet that fool by myself. I barely even like this whole idea," Snoop responded.

"Shit." King paused. "Well, Loc ridin with me today. We gotta grab this money."

"I feel that."

I walked in on King and Snoop as they discussed the logistics of the Toronto trip to check out the new territory. I missed the beginning of their conversation but I pretty much caught the gist. King and Loc needed to be in the city to receive this month's counterfeit supply. King was the only person that could sign off on the shipment so he had to be there. If he missed it we wouldn't have any weight to move all month. On the other hand, we had this big opportunity to expand our operation by meeting with Chino but Snoop couldn't make the run by himself because he had a conflict of interest. I shook my head at the dilemma.

"What you shaking yo head for?" Snoop asked me as I

opened the fridge looking for a drink. "You should make Pinky go up there. It was her idea anyway."

I mugged him as I took a sip from a water bottle.

"Actually. That could work. But you go with her. Keep my baby safe." King pointed at Snoop and looked at me. "And you make sure this fool don't do nothing dumb," he told me.

"Wait. Hold up. Who said I would go?" I faced King.

"You don't get a choice, sweetheart. King has spoken." Snoop couldn't wait to pull the King card on me despite the fact that he defies orders all the time.

"I'm not sure those rules work the same way for me." I snapped my neck. "Plus I wasn't talking to yo ass in the first place." I shut his ass up.

"Nah I need you to go, Ally. You know I wouldn't send you if I didn't have to." King spoke. He then grabbed his wallet, his piece, and his cell phone then walked out the garage to the car where Loc was waiting for him.

"Don't fuck nothing up. That's an order for the both of you." He made his final speech and let the door close behind him.

Snoop glanced at me then he walked into the living room and lay across the couch. It was still very early in the morning. The sun hadn't even thought about getting up yet. Since I was already up and in the kitchen, I made breakfast. I baked a pack of pork center cut bacon, scrambled a few eggs with green peppers, red onions, and shredded cheese, whipped up a pot of thick buttery grits, and baked four country style biscuits. There was always plenty of juice and fresh fruit in the fridge so I made fresh fruit smoothies to accompany the meal. I brought Snoop a plate on the couch and joined him with my plate as we watched some satire comedy show that Snoop picked out. Of course, he was blowed by now because he smoked the entire time I cooked.

"How are you fine and can cook?" Snoop asked with his mouth full, not looking up from his plate.

"I don't understand what looks have to do with somebody's ability to cook."

"Fine hoes can't cook."

"Excuse me?" I turned to look at him.

"Not saying you a hoe. I'm just sayin," he attempted to calm me.

"Whatever. I can cook because I like to eat. Simple as that."

The truth was I was learning as I went. I read a lot of recipes and watch shows and became adventurous in the kitchen. I also learned technique from my mom when I was younger.

Snoop paused on the questions and finished his plate. After we ate, he got on the phone to make a few last minute calls. He told me we were leaving promptly at seven. We had to wait on a car to be dropped off so we can make our run with an unregistered car. I went upstairs to shower and get ready. Snoop packed and loaded his armory. He also cleaned out his cash in his pockets. We didn't want to take any chances with getting robbed or running into the boys. I packed my piece in a holster and grabbed my backpack.

The drop off car was a brand new all black Chevy Malibu, dark tint, factory rims, and most importantly, a paper tag. Snoop walked out the back door; through the garage. I shut the house down and followed him to the car, locking the door behind me. We backed out, letting the garage door down behind us.

I hated the way Snoop drove. Compared to King he was way more rough with the road. He swerved through traffic like he was in a video game. I put my hood over my head and buckled my seatbelt tight; trying to zone out.

"Pinky," Travis pushed the top of my head.

"What?"

"We're on a seven hour drive. You have to talk to me," he demanded.

"What if I don't want to?" I was short.

"What did I do to you?"

"It's just weird talking to you sometimes."

"You know what? I think you starting to get nervous around me because you actually like me."

"That is definitely not it," I rolled my eyes.

He gazed at me for a second. "Yea it is. It's cool, baby. I'm not trying to use it against you. You already know how I feel about you. I been waiting on this for years."

"See that's what I mean when I say weird? I can't believe you sometimes."

"Because I tell you that I been crushing on you for a minute? That's not impossible. You don't understand how many men go home dreaming about you every night. You're a fantasy to most people. So yes, yes, I have been scoping you for years. If that offends you, I'm sorry. I don't understand why it does, but I am sorry."

Travis was always so sincere with me when it came to expressing his emotions. He had no problem showing me how he felt about me. It was so surreal because he was right. I did start to like him.

"I do like you. But I'm not nervous."

"What? You scared about King?"

"No, I'm confused."

"Tell me more."

"You don't confuse me. Your intentions are clear. What confuses me is King. He's so smart. He knows almost everything before it happens. So there's no way you been having this crush on me for all these years and he didn't know about it. King can read you like a book," I elaborated.

His face grew with tension, as if he was processing everything I said. He was careful with his next words.

"I think he knows." He didn't look over at me.

"What makes you so sure?" I was curious.

"The other day…" he started then he paused.

"What happened?" I was impatient.

"The other day I was blowing blunts with my brother and he made the statement that he saw how I look at his girl."

"And what did you say?" I couldn't believe he didn't tell me this sooner.

"I told him I didn't know what the fuck he was talking about."

"And?"

"And nothing. He looked at me then he moved on. See the thing about King is that he can read people so easily but it's almost impossible to read his ass. He's coldhearted, which makes it easy for him to hide his emotions. That mothafucka is the most dangerous nigga I know. He the last nigga I would even think about crossing." He looked over at me. "But, you. You the only person that ever made me want to cross him. I would risk my life for one night with you."

I heard the sincerity in his voice and saw the lust in his eyes. It was so refreshing to have somebody want me bad enough that they would risk it all. But King was one person I didn't want problems with.

"I think we both need to be smart about everything from here on out," I concluded. Travis nodded then he placed his right hand in between my hands which were sitting in my lap.

The ride was a straight shot to the Canadian border; a scenic but boring long ride. Just a few hours after we hit the road it started to rain. The roads grew slick as the clouds unloaded. Naturally the mood changed with the weather. Our journey started to feel more cosmic than it did initially. What seemed to be a business trip grew into a test of our emotions as the universe worked to change the vibe. I could feel myself growing closer to Travis. I wondered if he felt the same way.

• • •

Right at about two in the afternoon we passed through the border. The rain didn't lighten up one bit as we were checked for passports and identification. Our car was inspected as part of protocol and then we were on our way to complete our mission. Snoop made the final call to Chino letting him know we were about to pull up to the location he provided. Chino confirmed that he was still in position and Snoop confirmed our appearance. Upon pulling up to the location, Snoop parked the car a couple hundred meters away to check his artillery and ammunition.

"I don't trust this mothafucka. Never have," Snoop said to me once he noticed I was watching him.

"Why?"

"Cause he's like us. Street savvy snake. I don't trust him. So here's the plan: we approach him like everything is copacetic. Chop it up with him and all that good shit. He's going to introduce us to his distributors. Don't shake nobody's hand. Any gesture that says we agree with them puts us in a position of weakness. Don't do shit that gives up our power. When he offers us the deal, we will demand double. That's the plan, Pinky; you got it?"

"I understand. I'm ready." I pulled out my pistol, checked my ammo then placed it in my holster.

The meeting location was a huge warehouse that appeared to be vacant on the outside. I counted the number of cars as we parked. Seven. Seven cars meant that we needed to count at minimum seven heads when we got inside. I also peeped all the exits. Three visible doors on the ground floor. The door we entered faced south. The air inside the warehouse was eerie and freezing cold. The place was used to process cocaine. You could tell by the way the tables were set up, with no chairs and the low energy lighting lamps that hung from the ceiling. The warehouse's original purpose was for meat processing and storage, which explains the freezing temperature. It also explains how Chino keeps his money clean.

Chino stood in the center of the room, his crew was scattered about. Chino had to be about five feet and seven inches, barely taller than me and much shorter than Snoop.

"Nice to see you again, my friend," Chino spoke to Snoop. Snoop's face grew tense.

"Oh yea, I bet," he responded.

"Who's your pretty friend here? Is this your lady friend?" He was nosey as fuck.

"Naw, I'm a street runner. Nothing too major," I lied. I needed to keep a low profile.

"And do you have a name? Miss Street Runner," he continued to probe. I see why Snoop didn't like this ugly mothafucka.

"Let's get down to business. What you got for me?" Snoop changed the subject fast.

"See, I'm so glad King decided to do business with me. I have a lot of opportunity here from him. But I think the terms of our deal needs to be slightly modified."

"No fucking modifications. Now lay the deal on the table." Snoop had his hands in his coat.

Chino laughed as he placed a large duffle bag on a nearby table. "I've always liked you Snoop. I really do but this time we need to talk modifications. You guys want my territory to push your counterfeit bills. I have no problem with that but I need your team to start pushing our supply as well.

"Man, fuck no. We don't push white girl in our camp. That's not even up for discussion."

Chino started laughing again. "See this is funny because look where you are. In my territory. In my warehouse. And you walk in here like you run the place."

I watched everything and everyone in the room. Chino and his four men made five men in total that we could see. Which meant there were at least two other people in this building that could see us but we couldn't see them. I knew something was up. I felt like shit was either about to get really bad for us or we could flip this as a win.

"What do we get out the deal?" I stepped in. I needed to start talking to give Snoop a chance to start thinking. I also needed him to observe everything that I had already observed. So I took over the conversation.

"Twenty five percent of all profits, same deal I give all

my distributors," Chino answered.

"That's not a lucrative deal for us seeing that we operate out of the US. The travel logistics alone would put us in the negative. What other options you got?" I asked.

Chino looked impressed. "Street runner you say? You sound more like an accountant."

"I can do math. It's not that deep." I shut him up.

"Ay, Chino, do me a favor and have your two goons up in the rafters up there come down and join us." Snoop pointed as he caught on to the scenario.

Chino laughed, again. Then, he motioned his men to come downstairs and stand with the rest of the crew. Once Snoop could see everybody he pulled out his automatics, one in each hand. Chino reached for his gun but he was too late I already had my pistol sitting on his forehead. He put his hands up in the air.

"Tell your men to drop all their weapons or I'll unload this entire clip," I threatened.

After some hesitation Chino snapped his fingers and his boys followed suit.

"So I'ma say this shit once. And one time only. The territory that was promised to us is now in full operation by King. In return, we give you exclusive rights to all parts on the chop shop."

"And what about the Runners portfolio? That was a part of the deal."

"How I see it, after you just tried to juug me, I should blow that big ass dome right off yo midget ass body. Consider that part of the deal obsolete." Snoop protected his operation despite King's orders. "I'll have my people send you the paperwork." Snoop concluded.

"Now before you think about making any sudden moves, I'll have you know that we brought a little back up with us. Camped behind the north and east exit we got shooters ready to invade the moment they hear a single gunshot," I lied as I pointed with my free hand to the exits that I observed earlier. I knew we needed some security as we made our exit, especially since we were outnumbered.

Snoop and I eased toward the doors with our guns still pointed. Snoop picked up the collateral bag that held our agreement funds as we made our exit. When we got close enough to the door we made a break for it. Making it back to the Malibu without a scratch. Snoop started the car and skirted out the lot.

"Them mothafuckas was planning on putting a bullet through my head," Snoop exclaimed.

"It looked like they were planning on scaring us into accepting their deal. Too bad that shit backfired." I smiled.

"I gotta start taking you with me more often." I took his words as a compliment.

We bonded today. On a personal and professional level. We were getting even closer to each other and it felt so natural. Snoop was fearless, street adept, and business focused. Meanwhile I was a thinker, analytical, and perceptive. Together we were the perfect crook.

The rain refused to let up and the roads became impossible to drive on. So Snoop decided we would chill for the rest of the day and head back later. He pulled up to a five star hotel and copped a room under a counterfeit identification. He didn't wanna leave a paper trail of our presence. He left the duffle bag in the trunk and grabbed his leather backpack. He let the valet take the car but specifically instructed him to not touch his shit. I grabbed my backpack and followed him inside and up to the room. We walked into a deluxe corner suite. There were two separate bedrooms, which was surprising because I didn't expect that from him. But I appreciated the gesture.

"We only a few minutes from the border. I got somebody coming to meet us to take the cash and make a clean drop. But he gone be a minute. So make yourself comfortable," he told me as he came out of his shoes and his shirt. He was so focused he hadn't even looked up at me until he noticed I was staring at him. He looked good. His body was tone, fit, and chiseled. Unlike King, he had absolutely no tattoos. But his skin was so flawless that he didn't need ink.

"I'm about to shower if you wanna join me," he laughed, mocking me for admiring his body.

"Don't start, Travis." I rolled my eyes then went into my room and lay across the bed.

The storm continued to roar outside as I watched the water fall across the windows. I didn't realize how exhausted I was until I laid down. Before I knew it I was sleeping.

• • •

I woke up and walked out into the sitting area. Snoop was sitting on the couch wearing only sweatpants, covered in a cloud of marijuana smoke. He was in the dark with the TV on. The rain was still in full effect.

"Welcome back, sleepy ass," he greeted. I ignored him.

I took a seat right next to him and picked up the blunt out of the ashtray. My hair had been in a ponytail all day but after my nap it was down and wild. I was still wearing my leggings but I took off my hoodie and kept on my tank top. I was looking very basic but I wasn't tripping. I puffed on the medicinal stimulate and let my mind elevate. Snoop watched me smoke.

"What, Travis?"

He laughed. "Nothing, man. I can't just look at yo pretty ass?"

"No, you can't," I spoke with my lungs full then I passed the blunt.

"Well I'ma do it anyway."

"How much longer we gotta wait?" I changed the subject. I wasn't impatient I was just curious.

"Still got some hours to go. This the process. We can't take that much cash across the border so we gotta exchange the currency then have it deposited to an oversees account. The dude we work with is out right now tryna get the money."

"This is what y'all do every time y'all come out here?" I asked.

"Yea. It's the easiest run on the route cause we gotta spend so much time waiting. I literally just sit up, smoke, and chill."

Travis was so good about explaining the operation to me. He never held anything back. He only hesitated when he had to tell me about his personal feelings for me but even then he would let it fly.

He paused.

"You not tired?" I was wondering why he hadn't been sleep.

"As fuck. But I can't sleep. I get like that sometimes. You should help me sleep." He opened his arms up to me inviting me to get close to him.

I hesitated initially. But he looked so good and he had

been behaving all day. So I let him hold me close to him. He placed his arms around my body and pulled me near his chest. I rested my head right below his head and he spread out across the couch. My right leg lay in between his and my left on the further outside. His hands were low on my waist but he didn't grab my ass. I was comfortable. He was relaxed.

"Pinky," he said my name. I looked up at him.

Then he kissed my lips. The first time just to see how I would react; when I didn't move or look disrespected, he licked his lips and put them right back on me. He was a smooth kisser; gentle, passionate, and succulent. He interlaced his tongue between mine. He let his hands grip my waist. Just when I thought things were going perfect. He stopped. He laid his head back against the armrest of the couch and he closed his eyes.

He didn't try anything else. He didn't try to get me out my clothes. He didn't try kissing my neck. He just relaxed with me in his arms.

"Travis," I spoke to him.

"Yea, baby?" He answered me without moving his head and without opening his eyes.

I loved it when he called me baby. I don't know why. I just liked the way he said it.

"You're going to sleep?"

"I am," he answered me. "Why? You got something else in mind?" He knew I did.

"I mean… No." He caught me off guard.

"When you stop being confused we can do whatever you thinking about right now. I want you to be ready," He spoke calmly. "I been ready. This is not about me," he finished.

He held me tighter in his arms and then he did as he promised and fell asleep. I slept too. Listening to the rain.

15

A Stormy Night

Something about the sounds of raindrops hitting the window pane that seemed to calm me...

I woke up still in Snoop's arms. Even though he was on the phone, he still had one arm wrapped tightly around my body. I had no clue how long he had been awake but he never moved me or attempted to wake me.

"Yea we're stuck here for the night. Couldn't get enough cash. This rain fucking everything up." He paused as he listened. "Yea I got everything under control. I'ma take care of her." Then he hung up and threw his phone on the table.

"I'm assuming that was King." I sat up.

"Hell yea. Worried bout yo ass."

"You don't have to sound so bothered by that," I pointed out.

"I am. That nigga wanna protect you by any means necessary. That pussy must be fire," he laughed.

I shot him a sharp look. Sometimes I forget how much of an asshole he is.

"I'm just sayin," he tried to clean his last statement. He got up and walked over to the window.

"Can we eat? I'm starved." I asked.

"Hell yea. Let's go to the strip club."

"Really, Snoop? What's with you and strip clubs?"

"I don't know. I like naked women and chicken wings," he shrugged.

He went into his room to change.

"You don't wanna go?" He yelled at me from the other room.

"I never been to a strip club before. Well, I mean, besides Mike's."

"Are you fucking serious?" He popped his head out to see my expression.

"I am. The strip club is my job. I don't hang out at places like that."

"Pinky you missing out, baby. I'm telling you."

I wasn't surprised that Snoop was a strip club spokesperson. He made it seem like there was no other place he would rather be. I went into the bathroom to brush my hair back into a ponytail and check my face. I pulled my hoodie back over my head then I followed Snoop out to the car. He had taken his black sweatpants off and exchanged them for black jeans, a black tee shirt, and a black North Face jacket. It was still raining badly. The streets were starting to flood and traffic was moving in slow motion.

"So what happened with the money?" I asked.

"Dude can't get to me until the morning. The rain slowed him up."

I nodded. I figured as much anyway.

Snoop had me thinking about him so tough. After that kiss I couldn't help but wonder what he was like sexually. His lips were so soft. His breath smelled good, minty. His pace was perfect, he didn't rush it. And I loved how he gripped me with his hands. I remember watching him roll blunts one day and noticed how huge his hands were. He worked out often so his veins showed clearly on his hands and forearms. He was so cut up but he always wore jackets so I didn't get to see his body much. I loved how his hair was always perfectly taper faded.

"What you thinking about?" Snoop nudged me out of my fantasy.

"Nothing," I lied.

He glanced over at me.

"What are you thinking about?" I put the question back on him.

"You." He was honest. "You got some mad fire ass lips. Them mothafuckas so soft. I was thinking about getting head from somebody with lips like yours. Not saying it has to be you, I'm just saying." He laughed at himself. I laughed too.

"You really shouldn't have kissed me," I responded.

"Then you shoulda stopped me. But you didn't." He looked over at me. "I think I'm starting to make progress with you."

I hesitated to respond. "I enjoyed your kiss."

"Oh yea. So I can have another one?"

"I'll think about it." I played with him.

He nodded in contentment.

We pulled up to the strip club that Snoop didn't even bother to GPS. He knew exactly where he was going. We pulled into valet. The attendant opened my door for me. Snoop hopped out and dapped up the doorman then motioned me to follow him. The place was a large one story building, a lot bigger than Mike's. Upon entering, there was a small hallway where people lined up to pay for admission. Snoop bypassed that process. It was clear he had been here before.

When we got inside he immediately grabbed a waitress. I watched how he interacted with her. She was much shorter than him so he leaned over and spoke directly in her ear all while keeping his hand on her waist. Once she got his message, she escorted us to an empty booth near the center stage.

"Thanks, baby. Don't forget about me." Snoop spoke to her hinting that he was going to need her to come and check on us periodically. I didn't like that he called her baby but apparently that's how he talks to all women.

"Of course, you know I got you. I'll be back with your drinks and put your food order in." She was flirtatious. The waitresses at Mike's are like that too.

"You are way too familiar with this place," I spoke to him as she walked off.

"This my favorite spot out here. They got some bad ass hoes in here." I rolled my eyes.

"Stop being like that. You seen me in Mike's too many times not to know that this is my style. Don't get jealous now."

"Ain't nobody jealous." I wasn't sure if I was or not.

Our waitress came back with a bottle of premium vodka and a few mixer options. Then she brought out an order of fried chicken wings and loaded potato skins. I went in on the food while Snoop got every stripper in the buildings attention. He spoke to everybody and the girls that he liked he invited them to our booth. He had a few stacks of ones and he was generous with them. I watched the girls pull out all their best tricks, which was funny as fuck to me because they couldn't touch my skills on my bad days. Initially, I was starting to feel jealousy with Snoop's interactions but that changed quickly once I realized how much better I was. I could shut this place the fuck down if I wanted to. These bitches barely going home with a thousand dollars.

I finally became comfortable and just chilled, sipping my liquor. Snoop enjoyed his chicken and naked women. He seemed beyond content. He didn't grab on the women, like most men do, he just let them sit in his lap and dance while he smoked. He was so cool.

A few hours had passed by and I was starting to feel wavy. Snoop seemed like he had had enough plus his money was all gone.

"Let's go. It's past your bedtime," Snoop joked as he motioned me to follow him out of the club.

He made sure to say his goodbyes to his "friends" and they were sad to see him go. We got our car back and headed to the hotel.

After we got inside, I showered and changed into my lounge gear. Boy shorts and a baby midriff tee shirt, both pink. Then I lay in my bed. I was tryna stay far away from Snoop. He sat in the living space smoking blunts, of course. I became bored almost immediately. I wasn't sleepy since we slept so much during the day and there wasn't much to do other than watch TV. So I gave in and joined Snoop's session. He sat on the couch in his jeans with no shirt. I almost wished he was less attractive. I couldn't take it anymore. I gave in.

"Travis."

"Yea."

"I'm not confused anymore." I confessed.

He looked over at me immediately, just to make sure he was hearing me correctly.

"Come here," he demanded.

He laid back on the couch in a seated position opening his body up to me. I walked over and straddled his body. He embraced me. He licked his lips. I was nervous but that immediately changed after he placed his lips on my neck. I elongated my body as he pressed his moist lips repeatedly against my nape. He ran his thumbs over my nipples, through my shirt, which were completely erect at this point. He sucked my neck until he heard me moan. He then picked me up and carried me to his bedroom. The room was dim with subtle light coming from the street lights outside. He laid me across the bed without separating his lips from mine. Once he got me into position he liked, he pulled my shirt up just enough to expose my bare breasts. He rubbed his firm hands across my titties then he took them on one at a time. He bit on the meat and licked and sucked on my pierced nipples. He took his time, making sure to leave both my breast completely moist. I moaned uncontrollably, wrapping my hands around the back of his head. He then slid my panties off and parted my pussy lips with his fingers. He sucked all the excess juice from my inner lips then he ran his tongue against the length of my vagina. When he got to the clit he swirled his tongue and lightly sucked until I dug my fingernails into the comforter. He flipped me over, smacked my ass, then he separated my cheeks and put his face in between and ate my pussy from the back. His tongue was viscous and his lips were entirely too soft. I moaned his name as he made me bust on his chin.

He stood up and pulled his jeans off. His dick print pressed through his boxer briefs. His dick was a good length but it was thicker than average. He didn't even bother looking for a condom. He pulled my ass to the edge of the bed and forced his way inside me with my legs in the air. It was a tight fit, I could tell he enjoyed that because his facial expression changed. Unlike King, Snoop did not make noise during sex. He slow stroked me at first to give me a chance to adjust to his size. Once he got comfortable, he put his hand around my neck and beat my pussy up. Our juices intermingled creating a moist slushy noise. His dick was so thick that he never came off my clit. Before I knew it I was creaming all over his penis. He pulled out and smiled at me. I sat up on the bed with his legs under me. He lay on the bed with his hands behind his head. I thought he was done.

"Come here," he commanded. I shook my head no. I was wore out. "Bring yo ass here. Get on this dick," he demanded. His dick stood tall.

I followed his orders and crawled over to him and I sat on his dick. He filled me up immediately. He grabbed my ass while I bounced on his dick. I was so wet that he slid in and out effortlessly. My titties bounced with me as I glazed his dick with juices. He watched them. I decided since he thought he put it on me I was gone give him a run for his money. I spread my legs into a complete split while still positioned on his dick. Then I spun around facing the complete opposite direction. My ass sat on his chest as I rode him. He gripped my thighs, pulling himself further inside. Then he pushed me off him, came up behind me, and slid in from the back. He fucked me so hard that it sounded like an audience clapping with my booty hitting his abs. Right before he came he pulled out and covered my entire ass.

He got up and walked to the bathroom. I followed him. We got into the large walk-in shower together. I rinsed his nut off my ass. He grabbed me by my waist and pulled me into his arms. I wrapped my legs around him as he put his penis back inside. He fucked me against the shower wall as the water ran down our bodies.

"Travis!" I moaned his name.

"Tell me how you feel." He wanted me to express myself.

He stroked my spot over and over again.

"I love you," I moaned uncontrollably.

"Oh yea?" He was cocky. "Say it again."

"I love you, I love you," I spoke as he bit my bottom lip. I busted on his dick again.

A few seconds later he pulled out and busted freely in the shower. I wrapped my arms around him from the back and rested my head on his back as he washed himself.

"You don't love me, you do love this dick tho," he said to me.

"You could be right." I didn't want to admit it.

"So don't be lying to me just because I know how to make you cum," he said, turning around to face me.

"You told me to tell you how I felt."

He nodded. He looked mad. "Just don't play with my emotions."

"Are you serious? You been playing with mine all day."

"Nah, I wasn't playing. Everything I said I meant. Like I said, don't tell me you love me until you do." He made his final statement then he got out the shower.

I followed him, grabbing a towel to cover my body.

"And what if I wasn't lying?" I joined him on the couch.

"But you are so it doesn't matter." He sparked a blunt.

"I'm not."

"Oh and you just miraculously came to the conclusion while I was ten inches inside you. That's convenient," he said sarcastically.

"You made me say it, I can't help that I was in the moment."

He looked over at me. "Who's better? Me or him?"

"You," I told the truth.

"Who you love more?"

"You," I stroked his ego.

He seemed content with my answers as he blew his blunt still wrapped in a towel at his waist.

The rain still fell. The lightning struck and the thunder blared.

16

Two Sides To Every Story

It's always about who you know.

The drop went smoothly and before we knew it we were pulling up to the crib. Snoop spoke to me like he always had. Apparently our sexual encounters didn't seem to faze him. Me, I couldn't stop replaying the events over and over again in my mind.

King and Loc were both in the house when we arrived.

"Successful drop. Feel free to thank me whenever." Snoop let his ego show.

"Nigga thank you? I talked to Chino. Mothafucka said you set him up. I told you not to do no dumb shit." King was hot.

"That hoe ass bitch tried to pull a fucking ambush on my ass. He fucking lucky I didn't put a bullet through his skull!" Snoop yelled.

"Why would he do some sheisty shit like that?" King was confused.

"I told you that bitch was crooked."

King looked over to me for reassurance.

"It's true. He pulled up with six other dudes, had two of

em hidin with sniper rifles aimed directly at us. Then he tried to force us to push his cocaine product as a part of the deal," I spoke up defending Snoop.

King shook his head.

"That's why I hit the nigga for a juug. I promised the chop shop but kept the runners and in exchange for him keeping his sorry ass life, I took the five hundred thousand," Snoop concluded.

"That mothafucka not gone just take that deal without a fight," Loc jumped in.

"Then let him come through. I got plenty of shit waiting for him," Snoop added.

"Nah we can't off him. He's more valuable to us alive." King started to think.

"Yea alright, bro. Just let that bitch know I ain't the one to play with. That nigga tried to pull a gun on yo girl but you defending his life. Alright with yo backwards ass," Snoop rambled.

"What?!" King looked at me.

I nodded. "He tried it. Too bad I was already a step ahead of him."

"See! And you wanna keep doing business with the shady bitch. Man fuck that. I say we just off his ass," Snoop yelled.

"And then have the Canadian mob on our ass? That's dumb." King was right.

Snoop shook his head. "Man whatever. This yo business."

"The territory is good to push the bills in though, right?" Loc asked.

"Yea, that shit perfect. Cleaning the real cash gone be a bitch though. Our volume too high for the cash runners up there. We gone need to staff accordingly." Snoop knew his business.

"Good. That's something you can handle. We need to go-live up there with the next shipment, no excuses. In the meantime, I'll handle Chino," King said.

"Yea, you handle his ass before I do." Snoop had to have the last word. "Look I'm out. I'm running low on weed, I'll fuck with y'all later." He grabbed his keys, exited out through the garage, and pulled off in his Range.

King and Loc disbursed to handle business, they had a ton of shit to do. There was this month's new shipment that needed to be distributed plus King had to figure out what he was going to do about Chino and the mob. Shit was getting crazy around the home camp but the cash flow was going dumb. We had so much money coming in we couldn't get it clean fast enough.

Which was another problem King had to figure out. The cash drops from the distributors were piling up. I did my best to keep shit running smoothly at the crib since the boys ran around all day long. The business line stayed ringing off the hook with new orders for counterfeit cash flow. So, I created an automated ticketing system online with the use of some basic forms to capture our new business. The online form was tied to an IP address way out in the Midwest just in case we were being tracked. I pushed the business out to the applicable runners using throw away burner phones. Every three days it was a new phone. I sent Snoop the list of work daily just so he could be informed. He was mostly busy with picking up drops and cleaning money so he had very little time for the runners. This is where I helped. Loc handled the distributor business and King handled all the supplier details.

Besides the mix up with Chino, everything was running smoothly.

• • •

I had to work. Mike hated it when I had to take off so whenever I came back he'd schedule me for a ten hour or more shift. Besides the bar, I was his bread and butter and he made it clear that the business missed me when I was gone.

Tonight, I was on staff with Toya and Draya. Which was cool cause them the only bitches I actually fuck with in here.

"Ally, you be so MIA now. Yo ass use to work every damn night tryna get yo cash up. Now you in here like two days out the week," Toya opened up the convo.

"Maybe I got my cash up and now I'm just chillin," I responded while changing into my costume for the night.

"Be real, is that fine ass curly haired dude giving you the suga daddy treatment?" She laughed.

"If you asking does he take care of me, then yea he been looking out."

"Looking out so good that you whipping a BMW and shit. Brand new diamond earrings and yo ass been dressing mad cute lately." She bragged on me.

"I upgraded myself a lil bit. But don't get it twisted I still be grinding."

"Bitch where?! Cause it for damn sure ain't around this bitch?" Toya was being nosey.

"I always been a hustler, you know that." I kept it vague.

I dressed in a fuzzy bikini top and matching thong that was my signature baby pink with thigh high tan stiletto slouch boots. I was feeling exotic today so I asked Toya to Brazilian curl my hair and let it flow down my back. I was planning on taking a few mortgage payments tonight.

I walked out onto the floor just to scope the scene. It was barely midnight so the crowd was still light. A lot of the girls had just clocked in so they were out hunting for any dollar they could find. Talking and flirting with ugly men just to get their cash. The VIP was completely empty. I wasn't scheduled to be on stage until one but if we don't get any more customers I won't even waste my time on that stage.

Snoop was sitting at the bar. His usual spot, close to the corner. I approached him. When he saw me, he raised his eyebrows.

"I feel like you have a copy of my schedule," I spoke to him. I didn't take a seat at the bar. He turned in his stool to face me.

"Not at all." Then he turned up his drink and sat the glass on the bar.

Draya immediately came to his service, offering him a drink. The bartenders always wore boy shorts and a black crop top. Draya had big titties so she wore her crop top with a deep v-cut.

"Another one, Snoop?" She leaned over the counter showing her entire chest. Everything except the nipple. Of course that caught Snoop's attention.

"I'll take whatever you giving me," he smiled.

She smiled. "Well, I got something else you can have later." She flirted hard.

My face grew tense. I had never wanted to fuck Draya up before but there's always a first time for everything. Snoop turned back around facing me like nothing happened.

"So, yea, I'm not stalking you," he continued the conversation.

I paused.

"Here you go, Daddy." Draya did not get off the gas.

So I stepped in. "Dray you never treat your guests this good." I pointed to Snoop.

"Well, yea I only treat the ones I like good." Snoop sipped his drink.

"Oh that's funny. I don't see why you or anyone else would like him." Then I walked off in the direction of the locker room.

Snoop followed me.

"Where you goin?" He grabbed my arm.

"Getting ready for set." I rolled my eyes.

"You mad? About what?"

I glared at him. I wanted to be careful with my words. I didn't want to cause a scene. "You fucking her, too?"

He drug his hands across his face as he thought about his response. "Yea... I mean... I have. If that's what you're asking."

"So you just gone have me out here looking stupid? Who else?"

"Man no. It's only a few other females I hit in here."

I was furious. I didn't even know what to say to him. "What happened to all the bullshit you was talking about only being focused on me? How you just gone G me like that? You coulda been real with me. You a hoe who wanna fuck anything fine. You coulda left me out that equation."

"It's not even like that with you, Ally. Don't think that because I'm out here fucking that everything I told you wasn't true."

"Well none of that bullshit even matters anymore. I ain't a stop on your sex tour. Let's act like we never fucked and I'll go back to ignoring yo ass." Then I ducked off into the locker rooms giving him no chance to respond.

• • •

A short thirty minutes later and Mike's was packed to capacity. The VIP tables filled up and the general admission line was wrapped around the building. From what I could see, Snoop had left or at least he was lost amongst the crowd. I was first up to perform, promptly at one a.m., and my manager made sure I didn't forget it.

She found me every ten minutes reminding me "There's a full house tonight, don't make me look bad." Like I could make her ugly ass look worse.

"Welcome to the stage, the fine, the spicy, the chick who's nipples you wanna lick, Misssssss Pink Dolla!" The DJ introduced me to the club. I took center stage in my pink furry thong. Before I even moved I had the whole stage covered in thirsty grown ass men, waving their bills, begging for me to clap my ass in their faces.

I gripped the pole and climbed all the way to the top using my arms only. At the top, I did a flip hanging from the bars. Then I slid my fat ass all the way down the pole facing the audience. The dollars starting flying. The more money I saw, the more I shook my ass.

• • •

Tonight had been a long hard night but, it was worth every second. I walked out the building with twenty two thousand dollars of hard earned cash. I cashed out in the back office and exchanged my singles for bands. I made my drop at Mike's office and then I headed out. At nearly four in the morning I was exhausted. I carried my backpack, which housed my dirty work outfits, my makeup bag, my brand new cash, and, of course, my strap, on my back as I walked out the back door into the cool brisk streets of New York.

Even though it was really late the parking lot was still partially full. Mike's didn't officially close until six so there would be plenty of thirsty men in the club for the next few hours. As soon as I broke the threshold of the doorway a person reached out and grabbed my arm. Out of pure fear I jumped back nearly falling over a nearby trash can. It was Snoop.

"Man what the fuck are you doing creeping out here in the parking lot like this? If I woulda had my strap out I woulda banged yo ass." I was breathing heavily.

"You definitely need to keep yo heat on yo hip." Snoop attempted to lighten the mood.

"Why are you still here? Waiting on Draya?" I folded my arms.

He rolled his eyes. "You know damn well I ain't waiting on nobody but you." He started to walk down the parking lot. I followed close by, still working to get to my car.

"Yea that's what you want me to believe." I gave him a hard time.

He stopped in his path to turn around and face me. "You told me you love me. You said you wasn't lying."

"I wasn't…" I hesitated.

He continued walking. "When you love someone you let them explain themselves. You let them make it right."

"That's not how I love." I was still pissed.

"Then you don't know real love. Real love is forgiving. It's compromising."

It was so weird hearing him like this. He was teaching me. Can you believe it? Snoop? Teaching someone something.

"I mean. Honestly, I never been in love before. And the only people I've ever known to express love were my parents and I watched them fight my entire life. So... for me love isn't forgiving. Love is pain."

"I ever hurt you before?" We stopped at my car.

"Tonight." I looked down at the ground. Travis faced me.

"Yea I saw. I didn't like that feeling. I didn't like watching you be hurt. After you told me to leave, I left. I went home and I tried to pretend like that little stunt you pulled was some BS. I thought it was. But then I kept remembering your face and I could tell I made you feel bad. I don't wanna do that again. I care about you. I have sex with women all the time. And lots of em come to me pissed or sad because I don't give them the attention they want and I never feel bad for them. I couldn't care less. But you. Watching you in pain hurt me too. I'm sorry I hurt you. I love you too, Ally."

My heart sank to the bottom of my stomach. I never had a man tell me that before. Not even King. I felt warm on the inside. I could tell he meant every word out of his mouth. He lifted my head up by my chin and gently kissed my forehead. "Text me when you make it home. Be safe." Then he left and got in his truck. I got in my car, turned the heat on, and made the trip to the home I shared with King. I wanted to follow Travis back to his apartment and sleep in his bed, wrapped in his arms. But, my life is complicated. Instead, I slept in his brother's bed, wrapped in his brother's arms. My mind circled thoughts of him nonstop.

Me: I'm home

Travis: cool, ttyl

Shawn Flossy

17

Don't Get Caught Sleepin'

Just when I thought I could let up...

I learned more and more about the business every day. I was plugged into the operations workflow heavy because Snoop told me everything. Snoop leads operations. King is the CEO. King creates the strategy, vision, and execution plan. Snoop maintains the day to day cash flow. One cannot happen without the other and they feed off each other's vibe.

We were two weeks away from the next shipment, which wouldn't be an issue if we hadn't just acquired Chino's old territory. Snoop needed to start up an entire operation in a new region in just two weeks. He needed a solid distributor, a full runner staff that was double the size of the staff in New York, and some security.

King set his vision. He wanted to push major counterfeit bands through the southern Canadian border but he only wanted to hit low income areas and small businesses. He had to play it safe initially and not draw too much attention. Low income areas are known for criminal activity and wouldn't raise any immediate red flags. Snoop hated the idea because that meant the overhead for the operation was going to surpass the profit by well over twelve percent. He wasn't cool with the loss but King knew the loss would only be temporary. We sat at the roundtable to discuss.

"So you mean to tell me I can't get one major business in this new territory? Not one?" Snoop was standing his ground.

"Like I've said, no nigga. We need to play it cool this shipment. Next round I'll get you some bigger clients. For now, I need you to test the waters." King was calm.

"I ain't no "test the waters" ass nigga. We can get that cash up quick."

"You don't even have the manpower to run. I don't know why you disagreeing," Loc interjected.

"Yeah and I haven't figured out the automated ordering system for Canada yet. We're just not ready for the kind of volume you want," I spoke up after Loc.

"Man, I can have my shit together in two weeks. Y'all know me." Snoop put an emphasis on himself while he smoked his blunt. He hit it one more time then he passed it.

"Ain't nobody doubting you but we got a plan. That's the plan. Now stop bitching and get to work. This meeting is over." King got up and walked toward his office.

The rest of us sat there and continued blowing. That's how most of the round tables went. King said something, Snoop disagreed, Loc and I get one or two words in, King repeated what he said in the beginning, Snoop still disagreed, then King ends the shit. Wash, rinse, and repeat.

"Man, my sells about to look stupid this month." Snoop shook his head.

"Man, it ain't like you hurting for money, be easy, bro. Let's do this right." Loc passed the blunt.

"It ain't about the money, boss."

"What's it about?" I was curious.

Snoop looked over at me with his low eyelids. "The power. If I was running this shit it would be different."

"If you was runnin this shit we would all be doing ten to twenty in the federal pen." We all laughed.

"Fuck you, Loc"

We worked all day. Literally. Snoop and Loc ran in and out the house for ten hours straight, King locked himself in his office, and I ran through and organized hundreds of orders. Business didn't slow down no matter what we had going on at the home front. I collected orders, organized them by location, and sent them to Snoop. Snoop had his team running the streets. He was also recruiting heavy. He was street hustling, stealing hood niggas off corners and getting the lowdown on the upstate hustlers. He figured he'd recruit upstate runners and just have them travel back and forth, that way he could keep his eye on shit. Meanwhile, Loc continued handling drops and security. It was a long boring ass day but we brought in major cash flow.

Once everything died down for the day the boys took a chill pill and relaxed in the living room with a fresh bottle of cognac. You could tell they were drained because they didn't say much. They let the music shuffle through songs in the background, Snoop rolled blunts, Loc was half asleep, and King drank his liquor on the rocks.

I chose to use my relaxation time in my studio. I painted. I expressed myself through my paintbrush as I fluidly looped together a picture of three men "lounging on the couch." I was inspired by the team's hard work today and started to appreciate each individual role as a unique character. I expressed their personality traits via a picture. The focused and intense demeanor of Loc. The hardcore leader persona of King. And the diligent anxious vibes of Snoop. They were fluid yet unique. Separate while cohesive.

"Is that supposed to be us?" Snoop walked in.

"Supposed to be? No. It is you." I corrected him.

"Can't be. I don't look that pale." He pointed to his character.

"It's art. Doesn't need to look just like you, Travis."

"Oh." He still looked puzzled. "This is good."

"Thanks." I shot him a sharp look. I wasn't sure if he was genuine.

"You should paint something for me," he asked.

"Everything I paint is for the world. You can have any one of these." I guided his sight throughout the room with my paint brush.

"Naw. I don't wanna hear that artsy ass answer. I want you to make something only for me. Something dope. Sexy." He didn't look up at me as he lit his blunt.

I thought about his request. "I'll get back to you on that," I finally answered.

"Yea you do that." He puffed. "You going out to the city tonight?"

"In a little bit. We got a bullshit staff meeting at Mike's. Mandatory."

"Cool. Give me a ride? I left my whip at the crib and Loc bouta go pull up on one his jawns."

"Alright, I guess so."

He got up, walked unnecessarily close to me, then ran his hand across my ass. "Hurry up. I'm bored as fuck here," he demanded.

"Don't rush me!" I smiled as he left the room.

• • •

My car still smelled brand new because I kept my shit fresh. Snoop slid my passenger seat as far back as it could go to make room for his long legs and reclined the seatback.

"So you just gone get comfortable in my shit?"

"Yo little ass be all comfortable in my whip, feet all in the seat and shit and I don't ever say nothing to you!" He had a point.

I rolled my eyes.

"Why you didn't answer my text the other night?" He asked.

"Which text?"

"Don't play dumb, Pinky. The text I sent you and asked if you missed me."

"Oh yea," I laughed. He didn't. "I felt like you knew the answer to that, Travis."

"I know you do. I be wanting you to tell me though." He looked over at me.

"For a hood nigga you stay sentimental as hell," I laughed.

He shook his head. "Nah that ain't me." He paused. "I wanna hear it," he demanded.

I sighed. "I miss you."

"Now say it like you mean it." He played it cool.

"I miss you, Travis. I been missing you. Where you been all my life?" I laid it on thick.

He laughed this time. "Yo goofy ass. So what's the plan? I wait for you to finish with this meeting then we go kick it at my crib?"

"Or I can drop you off now, go to my meeting, then I go

home," I replied.

"Nah, my plan is way better."

"I'll kick it with you but only for a little bit, I got shit to do."

"Yea alright." He put his hand in my lap.

We vibed to some trap music all the way to the city. My speaker system thumped hard in my coupe. Snoop and I basically had the exact same taste in music so it was easy for us to ride and listen without talking. I weaved through traffic and he navigated through his phone while mouthing all the words to the songs.

Twenty minutes later, I pulled into a gas station to fill up my tank. I turned the car off, cracked my window, and turned the volume down on the radio. Snoop immediately hopped out the car and walked into the gas station. I knew he was going to go pay for the gas and he would have an attitude if I even attempted to pump the gas so I waited patiently. I was looking down at my cell phone checking my emails, nodding my head to the music until I felt a cold steel beam touch my temple.

"Don't say a fucking word or I'll blow yo shit off." The voice behind the gun spoke. I followed instructions. I didn't say one word. I dropped my phone in my lap and raised my hands in plain sight. Then a nigga in all black hopped into my passenger seat.

"Damn you fine," was the first thing he said. "What you got in here? You ain't got no designer handbags or no expensive shit in this fancy ass car?" I didn't say shit.

The voice holding the gun nudged my head. "Answer him! Where the money at?"

"I don't carry fucking handbags, mothafucka," I snapped.

"Bitch, watch yo mouth. You better have something in this car before I just have to take yo ass," the guy in the passenger seat spoke.

Next thing I know, the steel beam leaves my head and I hear the voice gasp for air, I pulled my piece off my hip and pointed it at the guy in my passenger seat. He threw his hands up quick. Snoop had the guy outside the car in a choke hold with his gun pressed against his forehead. The tables switched fast a hell.

"Who the fuck you think you are, bitch? Running up on us like that, with that bitch ass 38?" The man didn't say anything.

"Ay, bitch I'm talking to you." Snoop tightened his hold.

"Man, I was just tryna make some quick cash," he finally answered.

"You see the fucking license plate on this car? You see them two X's at the end? You know what that shit mean, bitch; don't fucking play me." I never knew the two X's had any significance.

"My bad, bro I didn't even check the plates! We don't want beef with y'all!"

"Yea I know, hoe. You lucky I didn't unload my piece on yo ass. You and yo musty ass homeboy can get ghost now, nigga. Don't let me see yo bitch ass again." He let him go. The guy took off.

"You can get the fuck out my car now!" I told the passenger I held at gunpoint. He hurried out and took off.

Snoop pumped my gas like everything was cool. I sat in the car with my head reared back and with my eyes closed. *What the fuck just happened to me?* After he was done, Snoop hopped in the car.

"Ally," he said softly.

"Yes?" I matched his tone.

"You ok?" he asked with concern.

I paused. "No."

"Come here." He opened his arms for me. I laid my head on his chest. He wrapped around me firmly.

"You know I'ma always have you back. Shit rough out here. You know that." Tears flowed down my face.

"I know. I'm just…" I paused. I thought about opening up more to him. "I'm just tired of having to watch my back every second." I raised up from his chest and wiped my eyes. "I'm tired of carrying my tool on my hip every day. The one second I think I can chill and check my phone is the one second a bitch catch me slipping. Can I live?" I asked as I cranked the car back up and pulled off.

"Nah, you can't live. Not like how you want. You got shit niggas want now. Nice clothes, a bad ass car. You fine so you know females hate you on the low. You can't chill. That's why I told you to always keep yo heat on you. Don't get caught sleepin."

"How you deal with this shit? You drive an even nicer car than this shit. You walk around with mad ice on."

"Shit I caught bodies. That's how I deal with the shit. I let niggas catch heat for trying to rob me. I sent plenty niggas to the chop shop. I got respect on my name."

"And double X? What's that mean?"

"It's my mark. We all use it. Niggas out here know that shit is affiliated with me. One X for me, one for King. We don't keep all them guns for show, Pinky."

It was at that moment I realized I was affiliated with some hardcore killers. I knew King and Snoop were criminals and I assumed they had one or two bodies between the two but it was apparent that it was way deeper than that.

"You safe with me. You in good hands."

I believed every word he spoke.

• • •

While we had our staff meeting Snoop sat at the bar taking Patrón shots and blowing weed. Mike and the two managers ran through their monotonous agenda. They complained about girls being late to their shifts, girls purposely forgetting to make their drops, and how we need to stop with so many free high premium drinks every night. I barely listened to they ass. I was just there to say I was there and so I didn't have to hear one of them bitch at me during my next shift. After we were done I drove over to Snoop's crib.

"I told you I'm only chilling for a little while," I reminded him as he ran upstairs to his room.

"Yea, I know," he yelled over the balcony. I sat on the couch, kicked off my shoes, and got comfortable.

Snoop came back down stairs with his shirt and shoes off. He kept his black sweat pants on. He grabbed the remote to turn on his background music then he pulled out his bong and sat it on the table. He took a seat next to me.

"You don't have to stay long, I just needed some alone time with you." He grabbed my feet that were tucked under my legs and placed them on his lap. He rubbed my feet with his firm coarse hands. I laid out on the couch and relaxed. I could feel his dick print under my calves as he rubbed my feet. His dick was big even when it was soft.

"Baby," he spoke softly.

"Yes?" I matched his tone.

"Come here." He gave me an order.

I sat up and climbed into his lap. I straddled my legs around his body facing him. He pressed his soft lips against my neck, slowly moistening my skin. His lips glided across as he interlaced his tongue between his motions. His hands roamed against my body. I moaned softly. I ran my hands across the back of his head.

He pulled my shirt over my head then unhooked my bra all in one continuous motion. He loved my breasts. They were easily his favorite body part on my body. He took his time caressing them with his hands, running his palm over them, and pinching the nipples between my piercing. He licked his lips. He picked me up by my waist, laid me on the couch, and pulled my leggings off. Then he slid his fingers around my pink thong between my lips to see if I was wet. I was drippin. He stood up and pulled his sweats and boxers off simultaneously. His dick was fully erect. He lay down next to me, grabbed my left leg, threw it over his waist, slid my panties to the side, and pressed his tip through both sets of lips. I clinched his back. He was so big he didn't really fit. He liked that. He slowly thrusted, loosening up my walls some until he could fit sixty percent of his dick inside. I moaned in his ear. He loved that. He multi tasked by sucking on my titties, gripping my thigh, and stroking my pussy. He stimulated my entire body. Our juices flowed. Once it got sticky enough for him, he started pounding. My body hit the couch cushion with every thrust. Before I knew it I was climaxing, screaming his name while digging my fingers into his back. A few strokes after he pulled out, he stood over me and dropped his dick in my mouth. Holding my ponytail, he fucked my throat until he filled my mouth up. I

179

swallowed every drop.

18

Brunch With The Slaton's

*Strangers treat you better than your own family
sometimes.*

King finally decided to give himself a day off. After months off nonstop eighteen hour days, he found some time for himself. I think he started to notice how stressed out he was making himself and that continuing to work wasn't making his output any better. It was Sunday, so work was going to be slow anyway. He delegated where he saw fit.

One of King's greatest qualities was that he never half ass did anything. Everything he did, he did at one hundred percent. So when he committed to relaxing that meant he was literally relaxing. He turned off his phones and stayed clear of his office.

"I forgot what it feels like not to work. It's been a minute." We lay in bed, it was barely seven in the morning. My head rested on his chest as his arms wrapped closely around my body.

"I'm not surprised." I wasn't. I can recall two times in the entire time we'd been dating that he wasn't working. The first night I met him at the club and the time he was laying low from the Feds.

"I'm taking you to Jersey today."

"Jersey? Why there?" I was curious.

"That's where my moms and the rest of my people at."

My heart dropped immediately. I wasn't ready to meet his mom. Especially since I was fucking both her sons.

"You think we're ready for that?" I was trying to find an excuse.

He laughed. "You ready. Don't act scary." He gently moved me to the side then got up and walked into the bathroom.

"I'm just saying that I don't wanna force anything." I yelled to him as he ran the water in the bathroom sink.

"Un huh." He basically ignored me as he brushed his teeth. After he finished he came back into the bedroom in his boxer briefs with his bare chest out. Every time I saw King's body I compared him to Snoop. They both were cut up but Snoop's chest protruded just a little bit more, Snoop was taller and his dick was wider. But King was covered in ink which made his sex appeal go through the roof and his dick was longer. I honestly loved both of their physiques.

"You're ready. You don't have anything to be nervous about." He attempted to reassure me but I was shook.

"But... like... I can barely even talk to my own family let alone someone else's. Plus, I've never met a man's mother before. What am I supposed to say?" I had legit questions.

Again he laughed. "You can say whatever you want, baby. It ain't no formula to the shit. Just talk."

"Ok but about what? I'm not exactly an ideal girlfriend. I'm a stripper that used to boost cars in her free time. Real talk, do you really want you moms to meet somebody like that?"

At this point King was rolling across the bed laughing his ass off. "Ally, have you met me? I ain't never had a legitimate job a day in my life. If I brought home some blue collar college grad lawyer chick my moms would think she the Feds. You good. I promise."

He had a point. He did operate a multi-billion dollar money laundering operation outta his living room. It was safe to say his family may have low expectations when it comes to occupations. Still I was fucking shook.

I started to get dressed while Aaron was downstairs. I didn't know what to wear. Normally, I'd wear leggings and my Timbs but I felt like I had to wear real clothes today. I've never wanted to impress somebody before. Most of the time I couldn't care less about what other people thought about me but this interaction was different in my mind. I wanted Aaron's mother to like me immediately. I put on this red sweater dress that King bought me a while back. The dress was slim fit so it hugged in all the right places and the collar was oversized so it was still stylish. I complemented the dress with a pair of brown suede thigh high boots. I left my hair damp from the shower and laid it into a high curly ponytail. I skipped the full face makeup and only did my eyes to set off my look. I topped the outfit off with my diamond earrings. I looked good. King was wearing a tech fleece sweat suit and his all black Timbs. I was jealous. I definitely wanted to wear my Timbs too.

• • •

We made the long ass drive to Jersey which wasn't as long as I'm used to since we live on the outskirts of the state.

The ride was scenic but boring. Aaron vibed out to some soul music, I could tell he was enjoying his off day.

Once we arrived to his mother's house I was immediately stunned. Her home was located in the middle of the country near the water. It was beautiful. The front yard spanned out over yards and yards of well landscaped land. Her home stood as a single story Victorian layout dream home.

"Yo, I thought you grew up in the hood," I asked Aaron.

"I did. I bought her this crib a while back. Couldn't leave my people stranded in the hood." After he said that I immediately thought about my mama and Jade.

"This house is gorgeous." I continued to be amazed as we pulled into the circular driveway. We parked behind a familiar white Range Rover.

"Snoop is here?" I asked.

"Hell yea. That's what it look like." King was nonchalant but that added an additional layer of nervousness for me.

Upon entering the house, I was immediately impressed with the decor. Fine marble floors, satin drapery, large archway hallways, and expensive art pieces scattered about. It was immaculate to say the least. His mother rushed Aaron like she hadn't seen him in ages.

"Son! There you are my love. How is it going? I see you brought a friend." She quickly drew her attention to me. After hugging and greeting her son she opened her arms up to me.

"Mom this is Ally. Remember I told you about her," he introduced me.

She immediately embraced me. "I sure do remember. She's stunning. Good choice, son. Well, Ally, you can call me Tam or Mom or Mrs. Slaton, whatever is comfortable for you. This must be so nerve wrecking for you, meeting someone's mom for the first time. But, no worries, you are welcome just like one of my own." She had said a mouth full.

I laughed in a sigh of relief. "Thanks, Mrs. Slaton for welcoming me into your home. It's gorgeous, by the way." Mrs. Slaton still had her hands cupped around my wrists as we spoke. I spotted Snoop in the doorway of the kitchen cracking up at our encounter.

"Thanks, love. My baby boy helped me decorate most of it. Have you met Travis? Let me introduce you to the rest of the family," she rambled.

"Yea, actually I'm familiar with Travis."

"Ok good. Him and his brother are very close. I would imagine you've seen him one too many times by now." We laughed. She had no idea.

I followed Mrs. Slaton into the living room area. "Well, everyone, I would like you to meet Aaron's female friend, Ally. This is her first family visit please don't embarrass me. This is my sister, Trish, our good friend, Eva and that's my little brother, Troy." She pointed as she introduced me to everyone. Trish and Mrs. Slaton were exact replicas of one another if you looked at them too quickly. They were both average height with pressed hair, even though Trish had a little less length, and they were both clean well dressed women. Their friend Eva was a super petite woman with a low haircut. She was already well into a bottle of Hennessy so I could immediately tell she was the outgoing one. Troy looked pretty much like Aaron and Travis. He was handsome for an older gentleman with salt and pepper hair cut into a low taper fade and he was in good physical condition.

After meeting with everyone else, I followed Mrs. Slaton into the kitchen and took a seat at her large island. Snoop was sitting across the way drinking cognac.

"I'm just going to go check on the food. Travis be a gentleman and keep our guest entertained."

"Anything for you mom." He was such a suck up to his mother. She smiled.

"Hi, guest." he spoke to me trying to be funny. I shot him a stale face.

"Pour me a glass." I slide an empty glass that was sitting on the counter toward Snoop and the bottle of cognac.

He laughed. "Rough day, huh?" He popped the cork off the bottle and poured me up.

"Why are you being an ass?" I whispered to him.

"I don't know. It just feels right." He smiled.

"Well could you not?"

"I'ma be easy on you. You look good. You never wear nice clothes for me," he observed.

"I never wear nice clothes for myself. I just wanted to look decent for you family."

He raised his eyebrows. "I never took you for the 'impress other people type'," he commented.

"Yea, me either." I shot the liquor in my glass.

"Yo be easy on the liq, this not the strip club," he laughed as he stood up when he saw Aaron walk into the kitchen.

"Say, bro, you think Mom would trip if I try to smash Eva? She been giving me that look like she want a young bull." Snoop spoke to King.

"My nigga when has what Mom thinks ever stopped you from fucking a female?" Aaron took a seat at the island.

"You right. I'ma shoot my shot. Be right back." He picked up the bottle and walked into the living room. He did that on purpose just so that I could bitch about something later.

"See, I told you it wouldn't be that bad." Aaron grabbed my hands across the counter.

"Yea it's pretty chill. Your family isn't all stuck up, they laid back kicking it."

"I tried to tell you."

Aaron gave me a full tour of the six bedroom, four and a half bathroom home. The hallways were wide Victorian style and the bedrooms were spacious decorated with large plush furniture. There was a game room, a library that doubled as a study, a den, a large living room, and a dining room that was adjacent to the kitchen. In between the kitchen and the dining room was a social space where the large island, where Snoop and I chilled at earlier, sat. Aaron said that the house ran him a couple million dollars and the decorating was almost double the cost of the home. He also said the maintenance was crazy high because there was so much land. But, he specified that he would only let his mother live like a queen and he wouldn't have it any other way.

We sat down at the dining room table to eat the meal Mrs. Slaton prepared for us. It was barely after noon so we had a brunch spread. She made sautéed new potatoes with herbs and lemon sauce, turkey sausage links, buttermilk pancakes, cheddar scrambled eggs, grilled honey barbeque chicken wings, and crawfish cornbread. We piled our plates up and slammed. Snoop had two plates, which was no surprise to me as he always ate a lot of food when I cooked for him.

The table conversation ranged from normal family catching up to when the girls planned on taking their next Vegas trip. Aaron was right, his family was cool. Much different from mine. They were loving, unassuming, honest, and, most of all, real with one another.

"So when you gone bring a lovely young lady home like Ally, Travis?" Mrs. Slaton spoke as we all started to clear the table.

"I don't know, Mom; I'm still tryna find my 'Ally.'" He looked over at me.

"Travis too busy laying up with strippers," Aaron injected himself into the conversation.

"Oh please, tell me you not still messing around with the little hoes," Mrs. Slaton was concerned.

"I mean, I like what I like. What can I say?" Snoop responded.

"There's absolutely nothing wrong with those women's choice of occupation but you seem to always choose the most messy females out the bunch," she continued.

"Well, there's actually this one that I think you might like. She got her shit together. She smart, hardworking, polite, mad pretty but I don't think she feeling me like that, Mom," Snoop added.

"She probably feeling you. She just doesn't know how to have you. You are a handful, my child."

I helped clean up the kitchen and then Aaron and I said our goodbyes. I thanked everyone and expressed how nice it was to meet each of them..

"Mrs. Slaton that was an amazing brunch, thanks for having me." We hugged.

"Oh my, no need to thank me. Anytime you are more

than welcome. Take care of my son and I look forward to seeing you more often."

Aaron gave his mother a hug and a kiss and then we walked out the front door back to the car. Once were about twenty minutes into our travel I checked my phone:

Travis: You know I was talking about you

Me: I can never tell. All the females you mess with

Travis: Well now you know.

19

Screw

*I once thought I knew it all. Turns out I knew nothing.
Everything was a lie.*

I woke up to the sweet sensation of a man's soft supple lips pressed against my moist vagina. He held my thighs apart with each of his hands as he swirled his tongue between my inner lips and my clitoris. I was stimulated by the surprise more than anything. He took his time finding the right tempo and speed to make me cream. My body grew excited, my back arched, my chest elevated, my toes clinched as I released my pleasure. Aaron made sure to lick up the mess in between my thighs then he got up and took a shower.

The clouds gathered outside making it apparent that we wouldn't see much of the sun. The house was calm. Too calm. So calm that it made me nervous. After my good morning wake up experience I found it hard to fall back asleep so I joined Aaron in the shower. He always took a morning shower between 4:30 and 5:00 a.m. Today was no different. His chest protruded out from his one hundred set push up routine that he did every morning. His abs followed suit. I loved watching him bathe because his tattoos fascinated me. There were so many that every time I looked I noticed something new. Today, I saw the vine of a long stemmed rose wrapped around an automatic gun. Most of his tats were symbolic and carried a certain level of depth.

I stepped into the walk in shower beside Aaron. He immediately embraced me and held me close to his soapy lathered body.

"You up I see." He knew he had woken me up.

"Who could sleep through a feeling that sensational?"

He smiled. Then he let me go and finished bathing. I started.

"What you got planned today?" He asked. He never asked me that.

"Um... not really sure. Thinking about painting in the studio since it looks like it's about to storm. What about you?"

"You know. Work. Going out to Toronto to see Chino. Straighten everything out."

"You want me to go?"

"Nah. I don't need you nowhere near him. I'm bringing Loc and another shooter with me. We gone be straight," he assured.

I nodded as I ran my hands through my hair as I washed it.

After my shower I put on a pair of black leggings and a black crop shirt with no bra. My shirt was so short that from the right angle you could see the bottom of my breasts. I ran the blow dryer through my hair for a few minutes then I left it out to air dry. I wasn't planning on leaving the house anytime soon so I was good.

When I went downstairs I noticed the house was already full. Loc and some new guy sat in the living room chopping it up with King about their Canada trip. And, of course, Snoop was in the kitchen eating grapes from a bowl. I walked into the kitchen around the island toward the fridge. He stared at me.

"Good morning." I was feisty.

He gave me a head nod. "Where's the rest of your shirt?" He laughed. I rolled my eyes ignoring him.

I knew he liked everything he was looking at. He always tried to play me when King was in the house. I ignored him.

"Can you make me breakfast? I'm hungry as fuck." Snoop rubbed his stomach.

"I don't know, I'm too busy looking for the rest of my shirt." He laughed.

"Stop playin."

"Anybody else want breakfast?" I yelled into the living room.

King came around the corner. "Not today, baby. We're about to head out. Got a long day ahead of us." He kissed my cheek, grabbed his keys, then walked out the garage door. Loc and the other guy followed him.

"Later, Pinky. I'll take breakfast tomorrow tho," Loc said on his way out.

"I got you."

The door closed behind them. Then we heard the car back out the garage and the garage door let down.

Snoop hadn't stop staring at me since I'd been in the room. He did that thing where he seductively watched me and I could tell he was imagining scenarios with me. Once I finally looked over at him. He opened his arms and motioned for me to come to him. I played like I didn't want to at first then I gave in. He hugged me tenderly with his hands low on my waist. I rested my head on his chest.

"I wanted to be with you last night." I broke the silence.

"You have no idea how badly I needed to hold you," he confessed. I looked up at him. "And you got on this little ass shirt. Looking real edible right now."

I laughed. "You just hungry." I remembered his request.

"Hell yea. Make me a plate please, baby?" He begged. It was cute.

"Ok fine." I gave in.

"But let's do it at my place."

"Your place? Why?"

"Because I got some business to tend to in the city. My place is closer."

"Alright I guess so." I went upstairs grabbed my coat and put on my black Timbs.

• • •

"So tell me the story about you and Draya," I asked while I cooked in his kitchen. His kitchen was chef style, unlike the traditional style at King's house. His dining area was directly adjacent to the kitchen with no walls separating the two. There were two modern designed steel and wood high rise tables in the dining area. Snoop sat at one of them rolling up.

"Man she been on me since day one. Whatever week she started, a while back, she came at me hard. Every time she saw me she was right in my face. She kept telling me a nigga looked good." He laughed.

"What you say to her?" I probed.

"I use to tell her she was cute too. She is. Then one day

she slipped me her number and told me when she got off. So I hit that night. Nothing major. I fucked her in my truck." He laughed again.

I shook my head.

"She knew I wasn't feeling her like that but she keep trying my ass."

"So any girl that give you play, you hit?" I gave him a hard time.

"Only the cute ones." He leaned back in his chair folding his arms. He knew I wasn't done.

"It's just like them hoes to throw their pussy at the fine niggas."

"Oh so you think I'm fine?" He smiled.

I laughed. "You alright."

I sat his breakfast in front of him. Three pieces of thick homemade French toast, scrambled eggs with American cheese, and four sausage links accompanied by a glass of orange juice. I joined him as the table with my cup of gourmet coffee.

"You nice as fuck in the kitchen, Pinky," he said, stuffing his face.

"You say this every time I cook for you," I reminded him.

He shook his head. "It's true. You almost perfect."

"Almost?" I was wondering what was keeping me from the title.

"Yea almost. You get jealous way too fast. You too fine for that." He was vague as he took a break from his food to sip his juice.

"I think I get jealous right on time." I played with the subject.

"You should never be jealous. Nobody touching you." He made me smile.

I got up to finish cleaning the kitchen and once Snoop licked his plate clean, I washed that as well. I felt like I was at home in his crib. Probably because I've been here so many times and it's always just me and him. If he did entertain other women at his place he covered his tracks well.

Snoop approached me with his arms opened wide inviting me close to him. It was still pretty early in the day and the mood felt serene. I let him clinch my body in his arms. His hugs were so therapeutic; since he was over a foot taller than me he made me feel protected in his arms.

He lifted me by my waist forcing me to wrap my legs around his body as my hands held his neck. He placed his lips against my neck then he ran his tongue up the length of my neck. I turned my head forcing him to stop licking my neck but placing my lips directly in front of his. He gently interlaced his lips between mine as he walked up the stairs to his bed. Once he got to the top he stopped kissing me and looked at me.

"What?" My voice was gentle.

"I'm about to fuck the shit out of you. I'm giving you the chance to change your mind."

"I want you to fuck me." That's all he wanted to hear.

"I'm just making sure," he smiled.

He sprawled across the bed still holding me in his arms underneath him. Once we reached the pillows he released my body. He hovered over me contemplating his next move. He gently lifted my light shirt exposing my erect pierced nipples. He ran his hand across both then he pulled off my leggings. He parted my lips then ran his fingers smoothly across my inner lips. He was doing what I like to call a pretest. This is where your male counterpart determines if you're as turned on as he is without actually asking. Hard nipples and wet vagina are usually the obvious tell-alls. Travis seemed pleased with the results because he immediately went to work. He exposed his eight pack by taking off his black undershirt then he came out of both his sweatpants and boxers simultaneously. He pulled the cover over his body then grabbed my thighs and slid me underneath him. He took his wide tip placed it between my inner lips then thrusted inside. I immediately reacted remembering the first time I felt his penis rub my clit. I grabbed the back of his neck firmly as he made himself fit inside me. His right hand held my left thigh up as his left hand pulled my hair forcing my chest to rise. The look on his face showed his concentration. He had one mission: fit his entire dick inside. Something that we weren't able to do last time. He wanted to stretch me to fit his size. Meanwhile, I enjoyed every second. He thrusted hard and fast creating juices that I felt run down my ass. Once he felt he had good grip he pushed both my legs up toward my face. He slid in and out over and over until his entire dick was inside and his balls grazed my cheeks. He broke his silence and moaned with his eyes closed as he explored every last inch of my insides. I couldn't take it anymore and exploded all over his penis. Travis let my legs rest on his shoulders then he grabbed the top of his headboard and pounded through all my cum. The whole bed shook as the headboard pounded against the wall. My moans blended in with the natural sounds of our intercourse. Travis was strong with lots of endurance and even though his body was sweaty you could tell he wasn't tired. He let go of the headboard and slid my body down to the center of the bed. He moved my legs from off his shoulders and wrapped them around his waist then he laid inside my pussy for a different angle. Next he dug all his fingernails into his sheets and pulled himself in and out. The whole bed moved as he fucked me. I dug my short nails into his back as he picked up speed. My toes started to curl as I moaned his name into his ear. Right before I came for the second time he pulled out and stood up. His large wide dick was covered in glaze as he stood over me. I turned around and put my ass in the air.

"Nah that position gone make me bust. That's the kill shot," he laughed.

I knew that meant he was ready to get his dick rode. He loved that position. He enjoyed getting fucked. So I pulled his arm leading him back onto the bed and straddled his dick. He embraced my curves with his hands. He positioned himself so that my titties were directly in his face then he gave me a jump start and started hard thrusting his dick inside me. I took over. I was sexy but firm on his dick. I bounced up and down letting my entire body bounce with me. He gripped both my cheeks spreading them apart making room for his dick. He closed his eyes and enjoyed my insides.

Then there was a heavy knock at the front door. We paused for a second then Snoop flipped me off of him and stood up on the bed to look out the window that is directly above.

"Oh shit. It's King." He started moving for his clothes.

"What?!" My face grew with tension. "I thought they were gone." I didn't know what to say.

Snoop slid on his jeans and pulled his tee back over his head. His dick was still hard but his shirt covered it for the most part. Then he threw my clothes.

"In there," he pointed at a door that went into a small office adjacent to his bedroom. A room I had never been in before today. Without question I grabbed my clothes and went inside the room. It was small. No windows but I could hear faint noises as Snoop traveled down the stairs to open the door. My heart pounded through my chest as I sat naked on a cold desk chair. I could hear Snoop open the door and I heard chatter immediately. I could distinctly recognize King's voice. But there was another person's voice that wasn't clear. I couldn't make clear of the conversation.

After about ten minutes my nerves calmed and I realized I had to just wait my time out in the small closet like room. Then I started to pay attention to my surroundings. The walls were bare. Absolutely nothing except for a calendar that was displaying the wrong month. There's a mid-sized file cabinet in the far right corner and a small office trash can in the left corner. Then, there's a small steel desk against the wall with two monitors attached to a single computer. I moved the mouse. The screen appeared. My head started spinning after I processed what I was looking at. What the fuck?!

On the right monitor, there's an electronic file with information on a person's height, weight, occupation and other personal details. The subject of this document read: Lawrence "Larry" Shaw. My father. There was an entire log on his every move up until the day he disappeared and then it just cut off. On the left monitor, there's four camera displays. The top left was a view of Mike's strip club, more specifically the entranceway to the locker room where every dancer had to pass through before she took the stage, changed clothes, or made a drop. It was a live feed. The top right corner was a view inside my old apartment. The room was empty now. The left bottom view was an aerial view of the block where my dad's barbershop is located. And the bottom right view is a live shot of my dad chained up in a dungeon-like room I've never seen before. He was still alive. I covered my mouth with both my hands as I tried to muffle my moans, fighting off tears. I was sure my pops was dead by now but seeing him chained to wall infuriated me.

Snoop forged his way into the room.

"We good, they're gone—" he paused when he realized what was happening.

"What did you do to him?!" I screamed.

"Wait, wait, wait…" he tried to calm me as I pushed past him with my clothes in my hands. I quickly threw my clothes back on, unbothered by my appearance at the moment.

"You've been spying on me?" I asked through my tears.

"No! I mean—" he paused and took a deep breath. "Ok, look, I'll tell you everything but you gotta calm down." He placed his hand on my shoulder.

"What the fuck do you mean calm down?!" Even though I was expressing resistance, I was calming. I needed to eliminate as much emotion as possible to get the information I needed and to get to my pops. I knew that he was alive but still had no clue where he was being kept.

"Just listen to me." Snoop was firm.

"You really not in a position to tell me what to do at this point. Give me the info and cut all the small talk." I reverted to my old ways.

He shook his head in agreement. "This is sensitive information, information we never intended on sharing with you."

"We?" I clarified.

"This was King's master plan."

"Why am I not surprised? That mothafucka only one around here smart enough to outsmart me." I insulted Snoop. He ignored my gesture.

"Larry Shaw, or as we know him, Screw, is not the man you know. He's a crooked ass ex-cop turned street hustling bitch."

"Ex-cop?" I was confused.

"Yea in the seventies yo pops was NYPD. One of the shady ones that busted into niggas cribs took their drugs and money and kept it for himself. He got caught up on some bogus misdemeanor charge and was released from the police force. That shit didn't stop him from being shady though. He spent nearly two decades busting into niggas operations and stealing dough. That is until he busted into Kings old crib back in Queens. Took everything King had, his money, guns all that shit. King moved to the crib you live in now a little bit after it happened. He sent me and my boys to find Screw. He was easy to find but not easy to catch. He stayed strapped and with his gang. You know them niggas that be at the barbershop."

"That's family though," I interrupted.

"Yea family to you but them hoe ass bitches was enemy number one for us."

"So why spy on me?"

"I was getting to that. Screw was hard as hell to get to except on the days you came around. For some reason he let his guard down when he was with you. So it was King's idea to get close to you to get the details on where he laid his head at night. When I saw you I knew exactly who you were. Ms. Pink Dolla, from Mike's. We started surveillance on the club. One night King slipped a slow-mo pill into your drink and waited for you to pass out."

"That day I had the blackout." I was astonished.

"Exactly. That night we found you in the bathroom. We dropped a tracking device in your backpack. Then dropped you off at the emergency room. It was only a matter of time before we knew where you stayed, the location of your mom's house, and where Screw stayed. We setup a camera in your apartment just to make sure you wasn't with him when we went inside and kidnapped him."

"In the all black unmarked SUV." I put two and two together.

"Yea." He reached into my backpack that was sitting on the side of the bed and pulled out the tracking device to confirm his story.

I sat on the edge of the bed with my head in my hands.

"So what else do y'all want?! Why am I still here?"

Snoop shook his head and sat next to me. "King commanded that nobody get involved with you but after he saw you that first night in the club he fell for you just like I did. King always knew how I felt about you. I been talking about you for years. Yet, he ignored that and started fucking with you. We was never gone hurt you." He put his hand on my lap. I got up and moved away from him.

"Take me to him. To my dad."

"Nah, I can't do that."

"You got me fucked up. As much shit as I know about

y'all operation."

"You not no snitch!"

"I'm also not a traitor. I'm not about to let you kill him!"

Snoop rolled his eyes. "Man I can't take you to him because we don't have him anymore. That was old footage on the videotape. Turns out he had a bigger tag on his head up in Canada. We did a trade with Chino. We gave him the "chop shop" in trade for a truce."

"Is that what you all meant by chop shop?" My confusion grew.

Snoop dropped his hands into his head as he attempted to make the story make sense. "The chop shop is technically a spot where we off mothafuckas but is usually referenced by others as the collection of wanted assholes, like your pops. We don't take regular everyday bitches to the chop shop. You cross us, you normally get murked where you stand but for those that we can get some collateral for we keep at the shop, for safe keeping. Turns out your pops was worth more to us than we thought."

"So is he alive or is he dead?" I need to know.

"I don't fucking know, Allyson. And to be honest, I don't care. That nigga deserves everything that comes his way." Snoop stood up.

"I can't fucking believe you and King set me up this entire time." Tears ran down my face effortlessly but I didn't make a sound. I experienced some relief knowing some details about my father coupled with the pain I felt knowing there was a significant chance he was floating in a river somewhere.

"Like I said, initially it was a setup. But you family now Pinky." Snoop knew he couldn't say much to win me over at this point but he managed to say enough that made me believe him. He was right. I had no one. My own family used me for the bare minimum bullshit that I did have, including my pops.

I didn't know what to do. I felt lost yet experienced clarity at the same time. I laid on the edge of Snoop's bed drowned in my own tears until I fell silently asleep.

20

Ghost Town

*Be careful when searching for the truth; you never know
what will surface.*

The next couple of weeks were hard for me. After
learning the details of our introduction, I stayed clear of
King and Snoop. For two weeks straight, I worked double
shifts and slept between the club and Toya's one bedroom
apartment. I couldn't face King after learning what I knew
about him and to make matters worse, I couldn't ask him
what I wanted to know without exposing my relationship
with Snoop. I had way too many questions to lay next to
King every night like everything was fine.

King called me two days after I decided to hide out.
"Baby where you been?" he asked me. I lied to him and told
him I was doing a favor for Mike and working a few
doubles. He was going out of town anyway so he couldn't
actually check on whether or not I was showing up at the
house. Unlike King, Snoop was completely plugged into me.
He showed up at the club every other night. At first he
played it cool; he went with the 'let me give her some space'
approach. Once he realized I wasn't going home he became

more vocal. Asking me shit like where I'd been staying and begging me to coming home with him. Like I wasn't having a hard time trusting him after all the shit that went down.

I walked back and forth down a busy street in the middle of the square. The last couple of days seem to blur together. One thing that didn't seem to dissipate was my responsibility to my mother. I didn't feel like traveling to my mom's crib but it was that time of month where I knew she needed money. My internal clock clicked and I felt compelled to visit. The last time I was there I nearly killed a stranger right in my mother's dining room. There was no telling what could happen this time. I went through my backpack checking for all my essentials, ensuring I didn't leave anything at Mike's. I couldn't take any chances with traveling back to the hood.

I took a detour once I hit Brooklyn, driving past Dad's brownstone instead of directly to Mom's place. I remembered he kept a spare key on the backdoor under the stairwell. I heard Snoop's version of 'The Screw' story and while the story seemed to line up, a part of me needed to know more. His grass stood tall as I shifted my way through to the back porch. After a struggle through the junk I was able to find his spare key. The same spare key that had been there since I was a kid. I traveled up the three wooden steps that led to his back door and peeled it open with the key.

The house was cold. A steel breeze waved through the back foyer through to the living room. Everything was in place except his recliner chair that was laying side down on the floor. I could tell someone grabbed him from the back, wrestled him out of his chair and out the door. I noticed the power was off after I tried switching the light in the hallway on. I walked through the narrow hallway that led to his bedroom and pushed back his door. The bed was made, as he always did before he left home to go to the barbershop. I rummaged over his dresser; his good watch and his work watch sat side by side, a pack of unopened gum, his wallet, and two speeding tickets.

I pulled open his top drawer. Under his socks sat two stacks of hundreds, a 9mm with no bullets, a bottle of hydrocodone, and a police badge. *A fucking police badge.* I grabbed the stacks of cash and stuffed them in my backpack then took a shirt out of his drawer and wiped my prints off of everything I touched. The handle to the bedroom door, the light switch in the hallway, and the knob on the door that I came through. I locked the door and placed the key where I found it. I slid down the alley and threw the shirt in the closest dumpster then walked to my car and drove off.

I pulled up to my mom's crib. Nobody answered the door and there weren't any cars in the driveway. I let myself in with my key. My nephew's toys were scattered across the living room. The kitchen was clean this time. I went in to my mom's room to find her laying in the bed.

"Mom," I yelled. She jumped up, frightened.

"Oh shit," I sighed out of relief. "I thought you were dead."

"Ah naw, child. I was sleeping. You bout killed me yelling my name like that." She sat up in her bed.

"Nobody answered the door."

"It's the middle of the day. Jade at work. Duke at school." Her voice was raspy. I nodded my head remembering it was midday.

"Well…" I changed the subject. "I brought you some money." I took the stacks I stole from Pop's crib and sat it on Mom's nightstand. "This should hold you over."

"Mama sholl appreciate you, Allyson. God is going to bless you, my youngest baby." She smiled at me.

"Mom, was Dad a cop?" I was blunt, skipping over her praise.

Her face grew tight. "A long time ago he was. A shitty ass crooked cop but he was on the force for a minute."

"Why didn't we ever know?"

"Because he was ashamed of himself. He got kicked out for abusing his power and then turned to alcohol and drugs to cope with his misery."

I shook my head as Snoop's story started to hold some validity.

"We could have been better parents, Ally, I can admit to that. We weren't the best," she attempted to understand why I was asking her these questions.

"Yea you could have," I agreed.

"We do love you though."

"Sometimes love ain't worth a damn thing. Sometimes the very people that say they love you will lie right to your face without any remorse. Love only works when people actually give a fuck about humanity. Saying you love me don't change the fact that I grew up on the streets homeless without anyone coming to look for me, care about me, or beg me to come home. Love would have brought you out of this house to pay your attention deprived daughter some fucking affection." Not a single tear rolled down my face as I poured out my soul.

"Allyson. We didn't know where to find you."

"Did you fucking look? Your ex-cop husband couldn't have found me? Where the fuck was my missing person's report?" I snapped.

"We did look!" She became defensive.

"Oh, well then you right. That sorry ass bitch is a shitty ass cop, couldn't even find a lil ass girl that was sitting out in plain daylight."

"Show some respect, little girl!" She started to share my anger.

"You, Pops, and Jade are my family but that doesn't mean we love each other. We did nothing but hurt each other. With all due respect, fuck this family. I'll be back next month." I swung my backpack across my shoulder and left.

• • •

I pounded my fist against the door to Snoop's condo. He came to open the door shirtless wearing black sweatpants. When he saw my puffy red face he grabbed my hand and pulled me inside then closed the door behind him. I followed him into the living room and joined him on the couch.

"Talk to me."

"You were right," I told him.

He looked over at me. "Why you been crying?"

"He lied to me his entire life. My mom too. Both of them been using me for money for years yet I never even knew who the fuck they were." I was distraught.

Snoop smoked out of his bong while he listened to my story. Then, he paused from smoking, lay his head in my lap, and looked up to me.

"You beautiful to me, even when you cry," he said to me. I smiled.

"Don't make me smile, Travis."

"I have to, it's my job to make you feel better." He sat up and opened his arms. "Come here." I fit snug in his embrace.

"I'm sorry you had to find out everything this way. I'm sorry I didn't tell you sooner." Then he grabbed my chin with his hand, raised my face to meet his and gently pressed his soft moist lips against mine.

"I never felt more alone than I did today. Hearing the truth after so many years just felt surreal," I opened up. Snoop sat back on the couch and listened to me vent. "Did you know I spent over two years sleeping in abandoned cars? My pops, an ex-cop, never came looking for me."

"I'm not about to speak bad about your father because I don't think that's what you need to hear right now."

"Well what is it that I need to hear?" I wiped the stale tears from my cheeks.

"That somebody genuinely loves you. There is somebody out here that cares about you. That one person, had they known you needed to be saved, would have come to save you."

I was touched, needless to say. Travis gave me something I never experienced before: genuine affection. I was more to him than the physical; I was a person whose life he cared for.

"I love you, too." I spoke without thinking. I meant it. Unlike the first time I told him I loved him, this time it was all from pure emotion rather than based on the physical. And then Travis did something he had never done before. He ran his hands across my back gently then commanded me to shower and get in the bed. He didn't try to have sex with me; just sent me to bed.

I slept that night under Snoop dreaming. Nightmares spawned and took over my brain. My mind raced, flashing between images of my father's abandoned home and the dusty Honda I slept in when I was homeless. My subconscious brain seemed to grapple with all the negative, looking for peace.

21

Foreign Visitor

Ten toes down; at all times.

"I need more from you." Travis spoke to me over the phone as I aimlessly walked around downtown.

I tried to get more details from him. "I just don't know what you mean by more."

"Don't play fucking dumb. You know exactly what I'm talking about." I could tell he was on the move too.

"There's just no way we can. It's not possible" It was obvious that, of the two of us, I was the realistic one.

"I see you're gonna leave this shit up to me, huh?" It was as if he was making a promise of some sort but his intentions were unclear. "Don't ever say I didn't give you the opportunity to come up with your own strategy. I'll see you later, Ally." Then he hung up.

I knew Travis was fed up with coming in second place after his brother; in relation to me and everything else in his life. He was the younger brother; the dope as fuck but not quite as good as his predecessor younger brother. The truth is, I'm not ready to make my decision on who I want to be with. I'm also not ready to face the consequences of choosing. If I chose King, I lose the person closest to my heart, a true friend and an amazing lover. If I choose Snoop, I lose my stability, my rock, and provider; and a soul that intertwined with my own. I had my work cut out for me. Not only did choosing mean I had to face the wavering truth, it also meant I had to hurt someone dear to me. While not choosing meant I had to watch Snoop suffer and let a lie linger.

Ever since I met Travis and Aaron's mother a few weeks back Travis has been hell bent on changing our status from fucking around on occasions to me being his girlfriend. He found a way to sneak the topic into every conversation we had. And after he proved his relentless loyalty to me by exposing my father and my family flaws, I felt much closer to him. I wanted to be his girlfriend but wasn't sure how that could work. He seemed to think everything would be fine but, it's Snoop we're talking about, he's not scared to take chances and deal with the consequences later. He's also not scared to defy his brother, never had been. But, me, on the other hand, I was terrified of crossing King. King was always dominating over my personality; he calmed me when I felt tense, relaxed my body with his dick, and touched my conscience with his words. King stimulated my mind in such a way that made me dependent on his energy. I loved how he restored balance into my life and made me feel at ease.

I went back home. Back to our home. King had been out of town for a week, I stayed with Snoop. But, I knew if I wanted everything to remain the same I had to go back to the home I shared with King to take care of things. Laundry, meals, shopping, and getting myself ready for my man's return. The house was a little stale from low activity over the last couple days so I had to bring it back to life. I was happy to be back in my own crib around my own belongings. I loved staying with Snoop just because he was there but I like being around and in my environment as well. There was something reassuring to me knowing that I could actually call a place my home. A place I never felt like I had growing up.

I slipped into a short black tight fitted strapless dress and a pair of strappy platform suede stiletto red bottoms that King bought me. My titties spilled over the top and my ass pushed the seams of the back of my dress. My hair was blown out and straightened, running down my back. I rarely wore make up and tonight was no exception. I conquered a lusty playful inviting look that I was sure to give off more than a welcoming vibe for King. Our home was clean and neat coated by a fresh scent of salted caramel that expelled from lit candles.

I waited for hours in the living room, flipping through channels until the door slung open and slew of men came through the back door. It was King, Loc, Snoop, and the rest of the crew. I was startled and immediately jumped up from all the noise. King walked directly up to me.

"Baby…" His eyes looked remorseful like he could tell I was trying to do something special for him.

"It's ok," I reassured him. I felt played but I also wasn't too surprised. King being busy wasn't exactly unusual.

He wrapped his arms around my body then kissed my forehead. "You know I'ma make it up to you. I gotta handle some immediate business tonight." I shook my head. I understood. King released me from his embrace and joined his team in the kitchen. Snoop mugged me from the corner. I walked through the living room, past the kitchen down the hall towards my studio.

"So you just get sexy as fuck for King, huh?" Snoop whispered to me as he followed me into my art studio.

"What's the fucking problem Snoop?" I was already irritated.

"You the fucking problem," he continued to whisper.

"I didn't do shit, ok. So calm your ass down." I matched his tone.

"You been with me all week and the first thing you do when King comes back is plan a romantic evening. Man, fuck you."

"King is my man, in case you forgot." I had to remind him.

"Yea, I fucking forgot, seeing that I go balls deep inside you every other night. I been taking care of you. Don't forget that shit, Ally." When he finished speaking he turned and walked back into the kitchen to join everyone else.

I sat on one of my studio benches near the window and dropped my head into my hands. It was hard juggling Travis' emotions but it was even harder hiding mine. This constant back and forth was starting to get old. At first there was this level of excitement and entertainment from balancing the two; that excitement just seemed to turn into unnecessary stress. A loud deep rumble blared from the front of the house.

I jumped up and ran to the intersection of the hallway, the kitchen and the dining room to see what was happening. The back door was cracked off the hinges as if somebody kicked the door in to get inside. King and Snoop were fully drawn, locked and loaded on a foreign man that I never seen before that Loc had hemmed up. Dude was Latino, maybe five-ten or so, wearing dark stealth apparel.

"Bitch, you got some nerve busting in my crib like you bout this life," King spoke calmly never taking his eye off his target.

The foreign man mugged.

"Say something mothafucka!" Snoop grew impatient.

"I was sent here," he finally spoke.

"So somebody don't give a fuck about your life I see. Who the fuck sent you?" King voice was steady.

The stranger hesitated to respond.

"Nigga nobody about to sit here a repeat these fucking questions for you! Tell us who sent your ass or I will cover these walls with your brain particles," Snoop continued to snap.

"I don't know! I was paid and then given this address." The man went back to silence.

King rolled his eyes in disinterest and frustration. "Man off this nigga, Snoop."

Loc withdrew from holding the man and without hesitation Snoop blew a bullet smooth through the strangers forehead. His blood splattered against the white wall in the dining room and his body fell lifelessly on to the glass dining room table. His thick blood leaked from his mouth covering the round table. I stood there frozen. Snoop returned his weapon to its holster and grabbed his burning blunt from the counter.

"Y'all niggas clean this shit up." King pointed to his flunkies in the corner. "Loc you know what to do with the body." Loc nodded.

Snoop searched the body for a cellphone before Loc

commenced clean up.

"Here. Make yourself useful and unlock this. Figure out who sent him." Snoop handed me the dead man's cell phone then he retreated to the living room couch, joining King.

They seemed unphased by the series of actions that just took place. They handled the situation so casually.

I took my order very seriously and went upstairs to King's office to figure out how to unlock an iPhone without wiping the data. It took me all of twenty-three minutes to cycle through YouTube videos and apply the hack. Once I had the phone open, I searched through the call log and the text messages. Most of the numbers weren't saved so I searched area codes on the internet. Newark, New Jersey? The last call received on the dead man's cell phone was from a caller with a registered phone less than thirty miles from our house. I read the text message from the number:

It's late. Break in take out King and his girl too if she's there.

My mouth hung wide open. I took the phone downstairs to show the guys. The body was absent from the dining room. The blood was nearly completely cleaned from every surface it touched. King was unhinging the broken back door.

"What did you find, Pinky?" Snoop asked.

I showed him the text thread. His eyebrows raised as he cycled through the last couple of messages.

"Fuck. Somebody got a hit out on Pinky, bro." Snoop snatched the phone from my hand and showed it to King.

"The phone number is registered to Newark," I shared my research.

"Somebody watching us," King remained calm.

"No shit, Sherlock." Snoop was condescending, as usual.

King snatched the phone and called the number. We waited as the phone rang.

He put the phone on speaker. "It's the voicemail."

"It's Hector. You know what to do at the beep," the voice on the line stated.

"Who the fuck is Hector?" Snoop asked through his Kush cloud.

"Hector? Only Hector I know is the one from the pawn shop," I jumped in.

King thought for a second. "Nino. Nino dropped the hit."

"Oh shit. That bitch still mad about old shit from back in the day?" Snoop asked.

"Loc and I shook him down a couple weeks ago. He was jacking our clients, fucking with our business. So, we cut that shit out quick"

Snoop pointed at me. "Plus you took his best runner from him."

"Nino wouldn't do that, would he?" I was confused.

"You can't put nothing past these shady niggas. Look like we got a visit to make," King spoke.

"Cool, glad we got that shit figured out. I'm crashing on the couch. I'm about to be in a Kush coma. Wake me up when you ready to make this play. That nigga Nino might just have to see the chop shop if everything add up."

"Real life, my nigga. Ally you should go to bed too. It's late, baby."

I listened to King's demand and retreated to the bedroom. After a night like tonight I didn't know how to feel. But, I felt safe knowing I had two of the city's most notorious killers right in the living room.

Ally

22

Moment of Truth

With one event, one moment, one word, everything could change.

This particular morning the house was calm. After a night like last the calmness felt surreal. Everything was restored to its original place and even the door was hinged and upright. The boys had yet to rush through the living room with their energy. I knew they were going to the city to handle business with Nino and the pawn shop first thing this morning.

I stood in the kitchen barefoot on the cool marble floor sipping a cup of coffee, waiting. My arms were wrapped tightly together generating warmth to my body. I was nervous about the outcome. Nino and I had a real friendship and I couldn't imagine him putting out a hit on me. But, to King's point, nobody could be trusted. I knew I was safe as long as I was in the presence of King and Snoop but Nino could be dead at this very moment just off mere speculation of him trying to kill me.

Travis walked through the back door. He was wearing all black, of course. Black sweats, black hoodie, black tee shirt under his hoodie, black Timbs with black laces, and a black beanie. His tall frame made its way through the kitchen toward me. He didn't hesitate or give it one thought as he firmly gripped my body between his arms. I quickly reached over his embrace to set my cup down on the counter then, allowed him to hold me. I wore a peach lace boy short and bralette set; I had completely forgotten how much he loved me in lace. He buried his face between the side of my face and my shoulder then he kissed me gently on my neck and my cheek. He slowly released me from his arms. He mouthed 'I love you' without saying a word with his soft perfect sized lips and I nearly melted on the inside. I smiled. He was sweet. Then, he walked over the fridge to grab his morning glass of orange juice.

"What happened?" I couldn't contain my curiosity.

"Nino sang like a fucking bird. Apparently, he knew Hector had it in for King but he said that had nothing to do with him. I still don't trust that shady bitch but we let him keep his life for a small fee."

"A small fee?" I made him elaborate.

"Yea, I want that Latin mothafucka Hector's head hanging on a wall before the week is up and Nino gone make the call. I'ma get down to the bottom of this shit." Then he walked over and gently pressed his soft cold lips against mine.

"King is going to kill you if he finds out." Loc was serious as he joined us in the kitchen after apparently lurking in the foyer.

Snoop looked up at him, paused for a second then nonchalantly responded. "I ain't worried about what King would do to me," Snoop responded confidently.

"I knew something was going on between y'all two."

"It's really not like that, Loc," I tried to clean the air.

Snoop gave me sharp look. His eyebrows turned up and his face grew tense.

"Nah, bro you got a death wish," Loc finished, talking to Snoop.

"Oh yea? Let's find out then." Snoop spoke. I stood there frozen. There was no way he was going to do what I think he's thinking about doing.

"King!" Snoop yelled out the back door into the garage where King had just parked his Audi. King appeared out of the darkness. My heart dropped.

"What, nigga?" King didn't like the idea of being yelled at.

"What if I told you I been fucking your girl?" He came right out and said it. King face was covered in confusion. He glanced over at me.

"What?" He wanted to confirm.

"I been inside your girl, plenty of times, and she liked it. But because she claim she madly in love with you she don't wanna fuck with me no more," Snoop finished, nonchalantly as if he had nothing to lose. His demeanor completely changed from when he initially came into the house.

King looked over at me. "So let me guess, this started around that time y'all took that trip to Canada?"

"Yep," Snoop confirmed.

"And probably been consistent with it since I'm never at the crib."

"Yep," Snoop echoed.

"My spot or yours?" He needed more details.

"Mine. Always," Snoop answered. I literally stood with my mouth open watching the two of them determine my fate.

"Well, I would say she should have chose you cause I'm off that now. I don't do community pussy," King was withdrawn from our relationship that quick.

"Nah, I pass on her. She didn't choose me so I don't want her," Snoop lied out of spite from me attempting not to claim our involvement.

"So, I don't want her and you don't want her?" King pointed to his brother. Snoop shook his head. "Then, Ally you can go. Take all your shit with you. Oh yea, that's right; you didn't come with shit." He hit me hard. "Loc take Ally to the city. She not welcome over here no more. That's an order." Then King walked passed me and down the dark hallway to his office. And just like that my life had crumbled.

Snoop knew his brother would choose him over anybody. He knew that as soon as he told him the truth it was over for me and that ultimately meant I never really had a choice. I could either have Snoop and deal with the abandonment from King or have neither.

I threw on the nearest sweatpants and hoodie, grabbed my backpack, dropped my car keys on the counter, checked my strap for ammo and placed it on my hip in its holster, then followed Loc out to the all-black SUV. I literally came with nothing and I left with just that.

Snoop watched as my pride diminished. I said nothing to him, I didn't even have the energy to give him a cold stare.

"Pinky, I don't know what to say," Loc said to me as he pulled off.

"Don't. Just drop me off at Mike's."

We rode the entire way in silence. Nothing compelled me to cry or feel sadness as I left what I thought I had behind.

This feeling of nothingness was all too familiar for me. I was comfortable in it. I literally spent years of my life with absolutely nothing, so, going back to just that made me feel assured that I was going to be ok. I had propelled backward, back to homelessness, back to loneliness, back to uncertainty and those were the only reasons I didn't cry. I had no time for tears.

"Stay up, Pinky." Were the last words Loc spoke to me before I closed the door. I didn't reply.

I stood in the midst of downtown on the same street where Mike's stood. The world seemed to consume me as it swirled around me in fast motion. I was back to square one. Back to the place where I started years ago. I didn't know where to begin; I had to figure out my entire life again.

23

The Legit Way

It's better to own your shit, that way nobody can take it from you.

"Girl, I know you don't want to hear this right now, but you shouldn't have been fucking Snoop in the first place. That fine ass Aaron would've had all my focus. Plus everybody knows Snoop is a hoe. Once a hoe, always a hoe." Toya was right, I didn't wanna hear that shit.

"Toya, you fuck your clients for cash in the backseat of their cars. You really can't call nobody a hoe." I just wanted her to shut up.

She rolled her eyes. "I'm just saying, bitch."

"Really don't matter now anyway. Neither one of them checking for me at this point. I just need to focus on getting my shit together and back on my grind at Mike's."

I had my work cut out for me. Toya was letting me crash on her couch but between her boyfriend and bad ass son I knew I wouldn't last there very long. I needed to secure a place. Preferably somewhere close to Mike's since I didn't have a car anymore. I had quite a few stacks tucked away that I saved due to not having to pay rent for nearly a year's time. My only problem was passing the credit check. My last apartment was a favor from my shady ass landlady but I wasn't trying to go back there especially since I been living good the past several months. I didn't have any credit and I didn't technically have a legitimate job at Mike's. Mike and I had an understanding since day one that my cash was off the record. I pay him his drop every night and then I was free to take the rest of my cash with me. No taxes, no deductions, all under the table type shit. Without a legitimate form of income and a steady credit history there was no way in hell anybody would let me rent an apartment; especially in the city. I was fucked.

Just as I was cycling through all my options in my head, Toya's boyfriend walked through the front door and into the living room.

"Oh so you the little friend that's gone be staying here for a while." He sucked his teeth as he scanned over my body.

I didn't like this niggas vibe at all. So, all I said was , "Yea."

"You one of her hoe friends from that dirty as club?"

This mothafucka was one handful of dirt away from resembling a homeless man, how dare he call anything dirty. "Ain't nobody a hoe, friend. I'm Ally." I tried to be cordial.

He laughed. "All of y'all little dancing bitches are hoes in my eyes." He scratched his head as he disrespected me.

"And what that make you? Wifing a hoe?" I shut his ass up real quick. He rolled his eyes and Toya walked into the room just in time to save her nigga from catching a hollow tip.

"Oh, I see y'all have met." She was smiling.

"Unfortunately." I didn't give a fuck. "Look I'm about to head out to the city. I'll see you later."

"You good? I can give you a ride if you're going to the club." Toya seemed to be a bit concerned.

"Nah, I'm good. I don't gotta clock in for a few hours. I'ma go handle some business." I grabbed my bag and walked out the front door. If it was one thing that I refused to tolerate, it was disrespect. I don't even let them thirsty niggas at the club talk to me crazy and I be poppin pussy for strangers.

I caught the train from Toya's place in Brooklyn out to the city. I wanted an apartment in that area and needed to start looking. For whatever reason, after living with Aaron I picked up the habit of having standards. Before Aaron, I would have stayed in a barren space in the middle of nowhere but now I wanted more. I wanted to be somewhere safe, or at least as safe as it could get for me. But, I needed to solve my credit problem first and I needed to do it fast. I didn't have very many ideas other than finding a way to get fraudulent activity that made it seem like I had good credit in the system. I immediately thought of my smart ass homegirl Navi, it's been a minute since we linked, ever since that Range Rover heist. I dropped her a call.

"Hello," she answered like always.

"Navi, it's been a minute, my friend."

"Definitely has but it's always a pleasure to hear from you, Ally. Let me guess you need a hack job? Alarm system? Garage? How can I help?" This bitch loved doing this shady tech shit. It was like her life calling or some shit.

"Not quite. I need credit." I was blunt.

"Bitch, I ain't a credit card agency."

"Yea I know. I need credit without having actually acquired any credit. If you catch my drift."

She paused for second, I could tell she was thinking. "Hmm credit checks actually funnel through a government database. Those type of systems require some tough hacking," she explained.

"Navi I know. I can give you a couple days to fig—"

"Got it. Ah guess it wasn't as hard as I thought. So what you thinking a 750?" She blew my mind.

"Bitch, you are fucking the shit! Yea, 750 will work. Damn, thank you!" I was excited.

"Don't thank me just yet. This little service of mine is going to cost you a band. I told you no more favors, Ally. A bitch got bills, too."

"Done. Say no more."

"Cool. You should be good. Give it thirty minutes or so and it should be reflected in the system."

"I'm transferring the cash to you right now, Navi."

"Pleasure doing business with you, my friend. Call me whenever." We said our goodbyes and hung up.

I made my way over to Mike's to see if he could help me with the other half of my problem. It was still pretty early so the club was basically empty. There were a few regulars there tending to their addictions but other than that not much activity.

I walked into Mike's office. I gently knocked first but then I immediately opened the door to see if he was inside. He was; flirting with one of our newer younger dancers. I wish I could say I was surprised but knowing that most of these girls got their job because they let this big nigga smash speaks volumes.

"Ally I'm a little busy right now." He failed to properly greet me.

"Yea, I can see that." I rolled my eyes. "I need to talk to you. Now." I stared at my unwanted desperate coworker.

"Jasmine, come back through in a little bit. Let me take care of some business first." She got up, walked out the door and let it close behind her.

"You not scheduled to be here until later. What's going on?" He knew the deal.

"I need a favor." I was blunt.

"Now look I done already decreased your drop. You my most profitable dancer but if I reduce your payout any lower I won't be making any money."

"No, not that. Not this time. I need to be on payroll."

"Oh fuck no I can't do that. I can't afford to pay the taxes on the type of money you make every day. No fucking way."

"Man I can't afford to pay the taxes either but I need to prove I have a job."

"The fuck for?" He was questioning me hard.

I looked away. "I got kicked out of my current living situation. I'm technically homeless at the moment and in order to get an apartment I have to prove I have a job."

"Oh I see." He pondered on my words for a second.

"What about if I hook you up with a spot?" He offered.

"Define hook me up? And what area we talking?"

"I got a this little spot around the corner that LaMonica was staying in, you remember LaMonica don't you? Cinnamon." I nodded. I did remember Cinnamon, she was around for about a year before Mike ran her off because she was tasked with being one of his side pieces and working for him. "I been paying the rent on that apartment since I signed the lease but you can take it over as a subleaser. You just need to be able to pass the credit check."

"Mike you coming through for me once again in the clutch. I appreciate this, I swear I do. And yea I'll be straight on the credit check." I remembered the favor Navi ran for me earlier.

"I'll do what I gotta do to take care of my bread and butter. Now get yo pretty ass out my office." I knew he was hiding his sincerity for me behind his patronizing but regardless I was grateful. Mike had been there for me through some of the roughest moments in my life and even though I knew he was using me to keep his club up and running I felt indebted to him.

"One last thing," I had a final demand before I left. He looked up from his phone. "I want the lease in my name. I want an official legally binding sublease. I can't have another person take something away from me. I can't," I finished my request.

Mike paused. "I understand. You got it."

24

Funding

Whenever I needed it, I got it. Good, bad or ugly.

There was nothing like the feeling I was experiencing. Free, on my own, financially liberated, making my own power moves, negotiating my own deals! I was running so fast for so long that I never took a moment to stop and think about how much I was accomplishing. I let my failures fuel me day to day so much that I lost sight of what I was fighting for. I had been fighting for my sanity and freedom since I was a teenager and now I'm here with both. I'm still missing love but at the minimum I had a small taste of what it was like to have people around me that loved me, even if it was short lived.

My new spot was quaint, comfortable and convenient as fuck. Literally in the heart of the city with an amazing view. I missed my art studio, the luxury king bed I shared with Aaron and our oversized kitchen. And I often found myself bored without my easel and paint brushes at my disposal but my current apartment is definitely too small for all my old stuff and is already furnished. I took to pencil sketching as a supplement to feed my creativity addiction.

I'm in a new chapter in my life where I learn to grow with the moments and evolve with the time. A viewpoint that's completely different than how I used to look at life. I feel like everything that happened over the last couple months, though hard, removed a heavy burden off my heart, mind, and soul. I spent years worrying about my father and mother but with my father potentially dead and learning the truth about my family I feel free. I'm not holding myself accountable for my mother and her home because she taught me one very important lesson: take care of yourself and yourself only. She left me to fend for myself in the streets just because I was the "problem child." She had all the resources at her disposal but never came to save me. She doesn't know it but that relationship alone made me who I am.

With this new chapter I'm fucking up shit; it's my turn to be on top. I learned two very important things from the Slaton Brothers: (1) Move like a mothafuckin boss, unapologetically and (2) Never get caught without my heat. I had a taste of what the high life felt like and I was determined to get it back. I was working on a strategy for my takeover. I wanted to build on my strengths. I have a few secondary strengths like carjacking, hacking, and stealthily stealing, just to name a few, but my primary strength is my body. I'm was racking at the strip club off my assets but eight to ten grand a night just wasn't enough for me. My next play needed to be an acquisition move. See, I read this article during downtime at the club one night. The article stated that in order to build wealth you need equity, collateral of some sort. I wasn't exactly sure what that was at the time but now I know it means I need to own the warehouse if I want to control distribution. To make shit simple, I'm taking the cash I normally shell out to my tired ass mother and ungrateful ass sister and buying a lot.

I spent my entire Saturday roaming around the city checking out property for sale. In New York, the property market is ridiculously expensive unless you run across a decent foreclosure. I had Navi hack into a few realtor agency databases and compile a list of all the foreclosed commercial lots in the city. Believe it or not, the list was thick, ranging from rundown shitty lots to high end retail spaces. I wanted something with a little taste and class but in an area that attracted the riff raft.

"Yo Navi, I need you to check out this place on the west side, 111th."

I had Navi officially on payroll.

"I'm on it" we both paused.

"Looks like a decent steal financially. Neighborhood not so great." She confirmed.

"I'm not worried about the neighborhood I got something for that. Just need to know if I can flip this spot."

"According to its public record there are minor plumbing repairs but the infrastructure is stable. If you like it I'd say get on it fast. Won't be around for long."

"Shoot me the direct number to the seller."

"On it." We ended the call and within moments I had the contact info for Andrew Coaster.

I had no experience with acquisition deals or making major purchases in general. But what I did have were superior negotiating skills and the toughest poker face thanks to working at Mike's.

I made the call.

"Hi, I'm looking for a Mr. Coaster... this is him? Great. My name is Allyson and I'm interested in making you a cash offer for one of your properties... yea sure... next week, your office... see you there."

Everything was running smoothly. Well, everything except for the fact that I didn't exactly have all the cash yet. But I had a plan for it.

• • •

"So run the plan down one more time." Toya needed reassurance.

"At some point tonight, I'm going to point a customer out to you. Whoever I point out I need you to dance with him. Get him extra hard, ready to fuck, then ask him to go back to his place. I'll follow you to his place. You keep him entertained and I'll take everything from there."

"And what do I get out this deal?"

"Ten racks."

"Deal. I don't know what you got going, Ally, but I could use the extra change so I'm down."

"This why I fuck with you."

I slid off to finish moving my chess pieces around. I needed to spot a victim. A rich one at that. There's usually some high rollers that come through the club every night, I just needed to spot the most gullible one and make moves.

I had to work a full shift this particular night. Which means a stage performance every hour on the hour. I paid attention to the crowd every time I was on stage, scoping out my perfect candidate. I finally found him in the back corner section. He was sitting alone in a six person section, which made me draw the conclusion that he had money to blow. He wore one piece of jewelry, a very flashy gold watch. I remembered King saying once that, "a nigga with some real money ain't gone brag about it." He was perfect. I moved my pawn, one of the bartenders, to double down his drinks and refill them without him asking. I moved my rook, Toya, up by a few spaces to have her start the initial seduction process. I slipped a picture of him and shot it over to Navi.

Navi: Jackpot. NY baseball player. Lives in Manhattan. Heavy surveillance but I can fix that.

Me: cool. I'll be making a move in an hour or so. Stay posted.

I watched Toya as I made my rounds through the club. She was doing just as I instructed. Thirty minutes in I could tell he was getting ready to want more than a dance.

"Yo, CoCo, you mind if I go on the stage before you? My turn right after yours."

"Yea it's cool, P Dolla. I needed a break anyway." CoCo was one of the extra thick strippers. A Thanksgiving meal away from fat. But she cool.

I took center stage early to give myself extra time between my next set. I clapped my ass for my two song minimum, grabbed my bills off the ground, then trotted my naked ass to the back. On my way, I gave Toya the signal to start taking our plan to the next phase.

I had between ten and fifteen minutes before Toya convinced our baseball player that it was time to head to his place. I needed to be in place to make sure I could follow them. Timing was critical. The only problem was the one major flaw in my plan; I needed a car. Mike was at the club and I knew he wasn't planning on leaving anytime soon so, I snuck into his office while he was out at the bar boppin with the bartenders. I went into his top left drawer, where I knew he stashed his keys, and "borrowed" them for just a little bit. It took me all of four minutes to make my way to the dressing room, slip into my regular clothes, grab my backpack, and sneak out the back door.

I was just on time. Toya walked out the back door with her new half drunk customer and hopped in his ride. I was already in Mike's car and ready for takeoff.

Manhattan wasn't too far from the club since we were located in the city. Our victim pulled his car into a fat ass Manhattan spot and parked and I watched him and Toya go inside.

I made my final call to Navi. "Yo Navi, everything is in play. What's the scene look like."

"I hacked into his home surveillance. He didn't arm his security system so there won't be any disturbances when you go in. The back door inside the garage is unlocked. Please tell me he left the garage door open."

Just as Navi was saying this I looked up and realized he was about to close the garage. I immediately hung up the phone, jumped out the car, and ran for the closing garage. Just before the door was completely closed, I tripped the sensor and the garage door stopped moving. I was cutting it close.

Navi called back. "What the fuck happened?"

"My fault, I had to stop the garage door from closing," I whispered as I slid on my belly under the barely opened garage door.

"Good. Explaining how to hack the garage would have been a tad bit harder. The back door is still open and per the surveillance footage, it looks like the bottom floor is clear.

But be careful; it's dark inside.

I put my headphones into my ears and kept Navi on the phone. She navigated me throughout the home as I tried to stay as silent as possible.

"There is an office through the kitchen, to the right." I listened as I made my way to the destination. "My guess is most of the tangible valuables will be there, except for the jewelry which is probably in his room."

I sifted through the desk drawers and all the cabinets looking for valuables until I ran into safe.

"Fuck. There's a safe," I whispered.

"I knew this was coming. Remember that stethoscope I told you to pick up?"

"Yea."

"Please tell me you have it."

"Yep," I confirmed as I pulled the item out of my backpack.

"Cool. Do I have to coach you through this one or have you broken into a safe before?"

"I YouTubed it last night. We should be good. Hold on."

I pulled out my headphones and placed the stethoscope over my ears and began listening for the clicks as I turned the safe dongle. I could hear every inch of my breath as I tried to be quiet enough to list to the safe. I just needed to listen to the pattern of clicks and once I heard a pause switch to turning in the opposite direction. After a few failed attempts, I got it!

"I'm in," I told Navi as I placed the headphones back into my ears.

"Yes!"

Inside the safe was several large bands of cash, a bag of

loose diamonds, a Rolex, several pieces of gold jewelry, and a gun. I took everything except the gun then quietly closed the safe and ensured everything was in its place. Then I got the fuck out of the house.

"Yo I'm out. Talk to you later." Then I hung up and called Toya.

"Hello," she whispered.

"You good? I'm outside," I asked.

"Girl, I'm coming. This nigga fell asleep before he even got it up," she continued to whisper until I saw her let the garage up and walk down the driveway. I hung up then pulled the car up to the curb.

"Please tell me you got the money," she immediately asked as I drove off.

"Man you know I got it."

"Fucking bet! Easiest ten thousand I've ever made. I didn't even have to fuck that lil dick mothafucka."

We drove back to the club and made our way back inside low key. I dropped off Mike's keys, changed into my outfit, and was back on stage for my next show. Clockwork.

25

Familiar Territory

Some things never change.

I robbed mothafuckas blind. That's how I funded my property purchase. I hosted two additional home invasions and ended up with over five hundred thousand dollars in cold hard stolen cash. And, since the money was stolen, I did my due diligence to clean it by recycling the bills through established businesses like Mike's. Took me a couple of long days to filter the stolen bills into Mike's organization ensuring that the bills I had in my possession were essentially untraceable to a single source of truth. I cut Toya the small fee of ten racks for her unwavering loyalty to the process and dropped Navi her usual fee for the navigation. And then, I met with Andrew Coaster.

Andrew was this stuck up white proper looking ass nigga. Just like I expected. Ugly ass suit that you could tell he had worn many times, tie that didn't match his button down, corny ass glasses that he needed to see the nearest any-fucking-thing, and a horrible Nice Cuts haircut that you could tell an uncultured Asian woman did for him.

Nonetheless, I was prepared to shell out my stolen fortune to him for the trade of a commercial building I would use to build my business.

"Mrs. Shaw pleasure to meet you in person," he extended his hand.

"Miss," I corrected him. I saw no need to be pleasant with him as I knew he would take my money regardless of if I was nice or not. "Glad to be here." I wore my poker face.

"Step into my office." He offered me a seat at his desk as he transitioned from his formal, clearly unsuccessful, greeting into his sales mode. "As I understand you are interested in my foreclosed property. I'd like you to know I have several other vacant buildings in much nicer locations—"

"I want the building we initially discussed." I cut him off. His job was to be a salesman. My job was to not get swindled. I remained focused.

His face became uneasy and then he transitioned back into business mode. "Awesome. That property's sale price is nine hundred and fifty thousand," he informed me.

"I'm familiar. I'm also familiar with the internal plumbing problems, historical annual property tax increases, and, as you mentioned, it's undesirable location." I flipped his sales pitch. "I'm prepared to offer you four hundred thousand in cash. Today."

"Miss— Miss Shaw, that's a little unreasonable seeing that I have others interested in this property as well."

I was familiar with other interest. I pulled out a stack of one hundred dollar bills and calmly placed them on his large wooden desk. "Are these others prepared to offer you untaxed, non-loan binding cash? Because this is my offer."

My face remained unchanged.

He sat back in his chair staring at the large wad of cash that stood tall on his desk as he thought about the trade-off of leaving a cash offer on the table. He contemplated hard but not for long. "Fine. It's a deal. I'll have your paperwork drawn up and title ready in a few hours."

"I really don't have all day, let's make it an hour and I'll add another ten thousand." My time was precious to me.

He stood up and extended his hand. "Deal."

It took a few weeks for the deed to officially transfer over in my name, to pass the time I completed my official LLC paperwork to formally start my business. My entire business plan was written on mental paper stored in my brain. I wanted to run a practical, profitable business and I also wanted to give back to my community. And though I completely funded my entire business through criminal activities, I followed my heart and opened an art center. A place where I could teach and practice my life passion and bring in cash from selling my pieces and expensive pieces from other artists. In my mission, I dedicated ten percent of all my proceeds to the women and children's shelters. I also offer one free lesson to children, of any age, that could prove they were enrolled in school. I had found my life's purpose and was moving quickly to fulfill it.

I spent the next several months, all of spring and summer, switching between building my business and working full time at Mike's. I was exhausted most days, running on barely four hours of sleep. But my motivation to achieve my purpose fueled me day after day. I woke up early, dragging myself into the kitchen to make breakfast and have a cup of coffee followed by a pitiful attempt to pick a decent outfit and sluggishly heading out into the city to put in work. Most nights, when I got back from the club, I would drag myself out of my clothes, leaving them wherever they fell and plopping into my bed. It was a cycle. Rinse, wash, and repeat.

"Ally you been in here every day grinding. I remember a time when you was coming in only two days out the week," Draya observed.

She was right, I was putting in mad hours. My business needed cash for various things; repairs, decoration, deeds, all that shit. And I had to fund it the only way I knew how.

"Yea tell me about it." I sipped my water bottle at the bar as I waited for my next rotation.

"I'm tryna get put on some of those jobs you had Toya doing for you. She said she came up big working for you."

I gave her a sharp look initially only because I wasn't expecting Toya to be advertising our work. "I don't have anything coming up but when I do I'll let you know," I lied as I walked away from the bar. I wasn't planning on doing too many more robberies unless I really needed serious cash. For now, the fifty bands I bring in weekly is keeping my operation in motion.

I nonchalantly strolled around the corner into the VIP lounge only to retract my movements immediately. It was Snoop. Sitting in the corner with a couple of other people. I peeked my head around the corner I hid behind to ensure I wasn't trippin. *Damn it's him*! I immediately went for the flight reaction and quickly attempted to walk past to the locker rooms where I could hide. But as I was trying so hard to not be noticed by Snoop I ran dead into a swole chest. I looked up, it was Loc. *Fuck.*

"Yo, Pinky! Long time, man." He opened his arms up to me. I gave him a hug.

"Hey." I was a little uncomfortable at first. Mostly because I saw Snoop get up out the corner of my eye and approach us.

Loc laughed. "Don't be like that. You know we all good."

I held my arm as a nervous habit. "Yea, I know. How are you?"

"Same shit, my nigga, same shit." He repeated.

"Yea I feel that. As you can see, same on my end." We both laughed.

By that time, Snoop was close enough that I could smell his cologne. I knew this was one of the moments I had been dreading for months.

Loc caught a glimpse of Snoop. "Ima holla at you later, Pinky." And he threw me the deuces.

I stood there frozen. Snoop sipped his straight Remy as he slowly approached me, glancing over my body. We faced each other. He said nothing immediately. It was almost as if he enjoyed my discomfort.

"What's up?" I broke the silence.

He shrugged. He didn't say anything. I became irritated, sucked my teeth, and walked past him.

"Same attitude, I see," he finally spoke. I paused, turning to face him with my arms folded.

"Same asshole." I followed. He smiled.

He opened his arms. "I don't get a hug?"

My whole demeanor changed. "A hug? You lucky I ain't tryna off yo ass."

He laughed, hard. "Man you couldn't off me if you tried. For one, your strap don't fit too well in that little ass g-string." He tried me as he pulled his shirt up exposing his piece, proving that he would have won the gun battle. I folded my arms. "You can't hate me," he continued.

"I can, actually."

"Nah, you can't. You hurt me first. I should hate you. I did for a while."

"I didn't do shit to you."

"Oh nah? You didn't have me fall in love with you just to tell me I could never actually be with you because you was too pussy to tell King the truth?" He opened up.

"You knew the job was dangerous when you took it." I rolled my eyes.

"You did too." He was right. I knew eventually I would have to face the truth.

"You took everything I had away from me," I spoke.

"Honestly, you didn't have shit. Other than a major dependency on my brother. I did you a favor. I gave you freedom. I also warned you that you wouldn't like how I handled that situation." Again I couldn't help but see the truth in his statement.

"I take it you doing ok. You look healthy still." He attempted to touch my face, I pulled back.

"I'm fine." I was better than fine but I didn't want to help prove his point.

Snoop grabbed my finger, pulled my arms apart, and then interlaced his fingers between mine. He stared into my soul and all my feelings for him came flooding back. He took his free hand and wrapped it tightly around my waist and placed the hand he was holding around his neck. I followed suit and allowed him to hold me.

He leaned in close. "I did what I did for you. For us. I

hope you forgive me one day."

Then I popped back into reality when I heard the DJ announce my name.

"Travis... I gotta work—"

"I'll be here. We need to finish this conversation." He says as he grabs his glass of Remy and retreats back to VIP.

I danced seductively in a hot pink satin thong with no top and thigh high stripper boots. I was a couple of thousand away from my daily goal so I made sure to pull out all the good moves. I was the only girl in the club worth paying attention to tonight, since it was a weekday, so the cash flowed in effortlessly. I kept my eye on Snoop; he pretended to not be paying me any attention but I saw him looking. His presence brought back all the old memories I tried to bury. I thought about that day everything went down and how much I hated Snoop's soul right after. But just now, smelling his cologne, being held by his arms, looking into his eyes past his long eyelashes reminded me why I took that chance in the first place.

26

Closing Contracts

That moment when the road takes a turn and you're not sure where you may land.

My days were so long; so long that they started to blur. Monday, Tuesday, and Wednesday all felt like the same day. The weekends felt a little bit different because the money at the club was longer but that was the only reason. After I had my initial exchange with Loc and Snoop, I made every attempt to avoid seeing them both. I realized the power Snoop had over me after just those few moments of speaking to him and I couldn't let him throw me off track. I was finally making positive strides in the right direction and didn't need any distractions.

Today, I am scheduled to do my walk through of my art studio to check out all the remodeling and technical changes I paid for to ensure it was operable. I was beyond excited. So excited that I even went out and purchased actual business clothes just so that I could look the part. I had never actually bought anything other than casual clothes and stripper gear so I spent hours in the mall trying on suits, dresses, and blazers. I didn't even notice that I had no clue what dress

245

size I wore until a sales lady at the department store asked. I gave her my pants size, which is in the double digits thanks to my ass but when I tried on the dress it was way too big. I ended up purchasing a few business casual dresses and two well-tailored suits.

When I entered the building, my building, to review the final product with my contractor I turned heads. The slim fitted all black cotton blend knee length dress I wore hugged every single curve on my body. And the stiletto suede pumps I wore didn't help. I was looking and feeling beyond confident.

"Miss Shaw," the contractor, Henrique, greeted me with a handshake.

I received his gesture. "Call me, Ally." I hated the formality of my name.

"Of course." Henrique was smooth. He had a heavy South American Latin accent but his English was impeccable.

"So what you got for me today?" I asked as he handed me a clipboard and a pen.

"Here's our requirements listing that we agreed upon initially for your remodel work. The first page is all foundational, such as plumbing and electric work. The second page includes all your feature requests such as painting, and the third page are extras that we completed while we worked on your defined requirements. The extras are of no additional charge for you, just something we do to ensure a thorough job," he explained.

I was impressed.

"Great. Walk me through line by line," I instructed.

"Absolutely." He led the way.

I spent my entire morning, literally four hours, walking through my building checking for perfection. Henrique and his team did an amazing job delivering to my expectations and beyond. The painting was perfect. The lighting was illuminating. The plumbing finally worked. My office was in a quiet corner on the second floor, perfectly designed. Everything was literally perfect.

"Henrique thank you so much for all the work you've done." I held his hand firmly as I complimented him.

"You're more than welcome. This is my job. Glad you are satisfied."

"You have no idea how satisfied I am. Allow me to treat you to lunch," I asked him as I sat down to give my feet a rest from the pressure of my stilettos.

"You don't have to do that." He was modest.

"I know I don't have to but I want to. Plus you've been having me run around here in my heels for the last couple of hours the least you could do is come with me to lunch." I smiled.

He laughed. "Ok, let's do it. But it's my treat. My father taught me to always treat a beautiful woman," he subtly flirted.

"Deal."

Henrique escorted me to an El Salvadoran restaurant only a few blocks down from my art studio. The area we were in went from questionable and sketchy to upscale in just a few short blocks. Which is one of the reasons I chose that location: perfect intersection of clientele. The restaurant was quaint but full of culture, eloquently designed, and decorated with original art pieces. I could tell by the canvas and the watermarks.

"I really love your vision for your studio," Henrique opened up the conversation as the host seated us at a table.

"You know something, I have been envisioning that studio since I was a teenager. I have been piecing the details of that place together in my head for a decade now."

"It shows. You're very particular to detail, which, as a contractor, I find intriguing because I am precisely the same way."

"What brought you to this line of work?" I was curious as I scanned the menu.

"Family business. Started by my grandfather in Brazil and migrated to the U.S by my father. I took over the operation fully a while back after my father grew old."

"That's dope," I commented.

"What about you? Art studios a family thing?"

"No. Not at all. My father owned, well used to own a barbershop in Brooklyn. I grew up in Brooklyn. I kind of had to make my own way with my career."

"Nothing wrong with that. I always wondered what it would be like if I didn't inherit the business. What it would be like to go to college and walk into a profession of my choice."

"Yea, me too. Always wondered what college would be like."

"Really? You didn't go?" He was so confused.

"Not even close." I was vague.

"I just figured a well put together woman like yourself surely had some sort of formal education."

I laughed. "If you would have met me last year, you would be saying something completely different."

"Damn. I'm even more impressed with you, Ally."

His comments hit me in a way that I wasn't expecting. Did he really think I was well put together? He really can't tell that I'll be shaking my ass for twenties within the next twenty-four hours? I was evolving right before my own eyes.

Henrique and I enjoyed each other's company for the next two hours discussing everything from differences in our childhood to most embarrassing moments. With the great food and the even better company time seemed to be nonexistent.

"Señorita, I really should head back to work. Need to wrap everything up with your place and dismiss my crew. It was such a pleasure to get to know." He politely concluded our extended lunch.

"Of course I understand. Thank you for everything." I spoke as we both got up from the table.

"My pleasure." Then there was a pause. A brief moment of silence that seemed to be occupied by both of our thoughts.

"So, since our professional relationship is kind of over at this point…" I started.

"I would love to see you again. Dinner, breakfast, brunch, coffee, honestly anytime of the day." We both laughed.

I gently pulled his cell phone from his hand. "How about I put my personal cell number in your phone and give you permission to use it when you're ready to see me again?"

"And if I just want to simply talk to you sometimes?" He also wanted to confirm.

"Then you can call or text me."

"Good. You'll hear from me, I promise." He kissed the back of my hand. "Until next time." He went about his day and I just stood there and watched his tall fine tone ass walk off.

I accomplished a major milestone for the art studio today but I also just became uncontrollably infatuated with my new Brazilian friend.

27

Slow Motion

Change is so consistent.

I sat in my living room on my couch roaming the internet looking for a social media page for Henrique as I listened to the rain beat against the windows. It had only been a few days since Henrique and I had lunch but, he's called me every night since. We were planning to have dinner this weekend, but I still wanted to see more and learn more about him. *Again, I'm uncontrollably infatuated.*

Do Not Answer : Yo

It was Snoop. I had damn near forgot about his ass with all the attention I'd been getting elsewhere.

Me: What Travis ?

Do Not Answer: Don't be like that

Me: ....

Do Not Answer: Come over

Me: Nah I'm good

I swiped left and deleted the thread, threw my phone on the couch, and got up to get ready to head to Mike's. I was scheduled for a weak ass day shift today. Which is normally fucking lame but is even worse now that it is raining.

Regardless, I was still a few months away from my grand opening of the art studio and needed to continue to make money. I packed my work duffle bag, checked my strap for bullets, flipped the safety, and stepped into my Timbs and North Face.

I normally would walk the couple of blocks down to Mike's but I took the subway to avoid the rain. Once I got to the club I immediately became pissed. There were literally three people in the club: a bartender, a bouncer, and the DJ. Not even Mike or any of the supervisors were there. In the locker room there were two other girls looking pitiful as hell because they weren't making any money. I took my sweet time changing into my all pink bodysuit and thigh high suede pink boots. Pulled my hair into a sleek high ponytail and went out to the bar. If I'ma be here I might as well get some drinks.

"Girl it's dry up in this bitch," Sadie, one of the new bartenders, started a conversation.

"Dry ain't even the right word. I'm lucky if I even make a fucking dollar today," I responded.

"I been here for four hours already and haven't made a single drink."

"Well, let me be your first customer. Make me a Ketel One martini. No olive."

"Cool." She started to make my drink and I chilled on the bar stool checking my phone to see if I got any texts.

"Nah you good, huh?" A voice from behind me spoke.

I turned around and of course it was Snoop. I rolled my eyes. "I had to work, obviously."

Snoop looked good, as usual, wearing all black; black jeans, black hoodie, and black Timbs with his gold chains hanging out. He looked like he was fresh out the barber chair.

He laughed. "Ain't nobody in here." He took a seat next to me. "I told you I wanted to finish our conversation."

"It's finished. I heard everything you had to say." Sadie dropped off my drink.

"Can I get you something?" She asked Snoop. She clearly wasn't as familiar with his favorite drinks as the other bartenders.

"Yea, baby hook me up with Remy on the rocks. Double." He threw some money on the bar.

Sadie made his drink then went back to being bored.

"I wasn't finished though," he continued the conversation.

"What else could you possibly have left to say?"

"I'll tell you but I don't want to tell you here."

I rolled my eyes. "I don't have time for this." I stood up and attempted to walk away. He grabbed his drink and followed.

"Yea alright cause you clearly busy as hell up in here," he said sarcastically.

"I'm on the clock, regardless," I tried to redeem myself.

"No the fuck you are not. Y'all get paid in tips not hourly." He shook his head.

I stopped walking. "Ok fine. I'll hear you out. Then will you leave me alone?"

He sipped his drink and nodded his head simultaneously. "Go change and meet me in the parking lot."

I listened. If I knew anything about Travis I knew that he was persistent and no matter how much resistance I put up he wasn't going to stop until he felt like he met his goal.

I walked out the back door to be met by a barricade of rain and wind. The storm wasn't letting up anytime soon which meant I could literally leave and not miss out on much action at the club. Snoop pulled his SUV up to the back door and I hopped in. It was almost surreal being back in this car after months of thinking I would never see either one of the Slaton brothers again. I immediately thought about Aaron. He literally had made zero attempts to get in contact with me nor have I seen him at the club or anywhere else for that matter. But, at the same time, that didn't surprise me because he was always low key. Snoop drove off.

"How's King?" I hesitated to ask.

"Really, that's the first question you ask me?" Snoop looked pissed then he saw my face. He could tell it was a genuine question because I literally got no closure from that relationship.

"He's cool. You know, just working. Same shit." He seemed jealous. "You got any more questions?"

"How are you?" I flipped the subject.

"You want to know for real?" I nodded. "Miserable as fuck." I wasn't expecting that answer. "King been working the whole team like a bitch. He barely can even look at me in my eyes. We don't get no breaks unless he outta town. I been making those boring ass trips to Canada by myself. I ain't getting no pussy. Life is trash."

I laughed a little. "Karma paying you a visit?"

"Hell yea. What about you?"

"Um, I'm not doing too bad. Working a lot more but by choice. Trying to stay busy." I chose not to tell him all the details.

"You fucking somebody else?" He didn't even hesitate.

I rolled my eyes. "I'm not."

"Good," he said as he pulled into the parking space in front of his crib.

We both exited the car and ran the short distance to the door to hurry out of the rain. Snoop unlocked the door and we walked into his cold, dark apartment. All the feelings I harbored in this place started to rush me. I remembered the first time we had sex here, all the times we snuck off here to get some alone time from King or Mike's, and the time I found out about my father.

We both took our wet Timbs off at the door and I dropped my bag and laid my North Face on top. Snoop went into his kitchen and poured two drinks then headed into the living room. I followed him. After he handed me a glass, he set his on the glass table in front of us and checked the bong for marijuana. Same Snoop.

"So what was this huge secret you need to tell me?" I asked as he filled the top chamber of his bong with smoke then cleared it.

"It's not a secret." He continued to smoke.

"So…" I probed.

He paused. Sipped his drink then reared back on the couch to enjoy his new high.

"I love you." He looked over at me. "And I'm not about to stop anytime soon."

I rolled my eyes. "You could have told me that at the club Travis."

"I want you back. Or I want you for the first time. However you look at it. I'm not going to be happy without you. You know I been in love with you forever and I couldn't just sit back and let my brother have the love of my life. I did what I had to do, regardless if it was ugly or not. Only thing that matters to me, is me and you."

I took in his words, thoroughly listening. He has been telling me for a while now that he's been in love with me for years and he is continuing to prove his loyalty through consistency. Yet I was still weary.

"Travis—"

He didn't even let me respond. He pressed his lips against mine and I just fell into his arms. I allowed him to grip and hold whatever he wanted. He held my body with passion as we interlaced our lips between one another's. Travis' passion was always well contained even when he was clearly excited. He perfectly placed his energy into making me feel wanted. His lips softly ran across the nape of my neck, kissing every exposed piece of my body. With his hands he pulled me out of my tights all while laying lengthwise against the couch pulling me on top of him. After my tights were off I straddled his dick in my black lace thong. He pulled my t-shirt over my head and then unhooked my bra without taking a pause from gently kissing my neck. I moaned. His lips were so soft.

He stopped for a second to sit up and take off his hoodie and shirt. His abs, chest, and traps were toned to perfection. His caramel skin glistened even in the dim light. He pulled his solid penis from his Polo boxers and then he came back to me.

"Ima make you remember why you was hooked."

That was all he said right before he started sucking on my tender already erect nipples. I grabbed the top of his head while I moaned as he pleased my pierced areolas. He slid his dick between my soaking wet pussy lips and I immediately shrilled his name.

"Yea, I know." He was confident. "Now show me how much you miss me." He demanded I bounce my ass on his dick. I followed instruction and allowed his inches to fill me up as I slid on and off with force. He gripped my ass, guiding my motions all while leaving my breasts the focal point of his mouth. I rode his dick up until he took full control of my waist and thrusted himself inside. He was particular about sliding his shaft against my clitoris with every stroke. I was loud. He flipped me over onto my back and savagely beat my shit up. I dug my nails into his back as I lost control of my body fluid and release secretion all over his penis. He pulled out right after I came and flipped me over; ass up. I knew that meant, it was his turn when he was ready for back shots. My pussy was relaxed, fully open and soaking wet at this point. Travis wasted no time sliding back in and gripping my ass as he got off. My ass fluidly bounced against his pelvic region and before I knew it I felt his nut running between my lips on to the couch. He pulled out and caught his breath.

I looked over at him in such a bittersweet way. My body was completely relaxed from the orgasm but did he just shoot his load inside of me?

"So what? You just forgot to pull out?" I tried to rationalize the situation.

He looked confused for a second. Then he started to put his boxers back on.

"Excuse me?" I reiterated.

"Chill. I'm thinking. Nah, I didn't forget. I just wasn't thinking about it at the time." He was super calm.

"Nigga what? You wasn't thinking about it? At the time?"

"You heard me." He stood up, finished the shot left in his cup, then walked up his stairs to his bathroom.

"Well are you thinking about it now?" I picked up my clothes and followed him ass naked.

"Obviously." He was so nonchalant.

"Travis."

"Allyson, chill. It's been all of two minutes. What's the problem anyway? I fuck you raw every time."

"Yes and you normally pull out."

"Yea but you mine now. I didn't wanna pull out."

"Oh so now it's 'you didn't want to'? Ok and then what happens if we have a baby? Because I don't know if you passed biology or not but that's the next step?"

"If we do then we do. If we don't then it's whatever. What's the problem?"

"The problem is that you talk to me about that shit first! We weren't even talking to each other a couple hours ago and now I might be carrying your seed."

He hopped in his walk in shower as we discussed.

"As I see it, you mine. It's been like that. I just let you cool off these last couple months. But I'm never strapping up to have sex with you and it feels better if I don't pull out." He spoke over the water.

"You should have talked to me about it first!"

"You right." He just wanted me to shut up.

"So don't trip if I take a Plan B or get an abortion." I tried to ease that into the conversation.

Snoop turned off the water and stepped out the shower. "Don't fucking play with me, Ally." He dried off and I got in the shower.

"You the one playin."

"You trippin because I don't mind you being the mother of my kids? You mad because I ain't tryna be with nobody else?"

"No, I'm pissed because you made a life changing decision for *my* life without talking to me!" I couldn't believe he didn't understand that.

He walked out the bathroom and I took the next two minutes to finish showering. I jumped out, stole a tee from his closet, and went downstairs to finish the conversation. Snoop stood in the kitchen smoking a blunt all casual. He looked up at me.

"You good now?" He asked.

"Did we solve anything?" I asked.

"You know I'ma take care of you. That's not an issue. You probably not even pregnant. I did pass biology and you would have to be ovulating to be pregnant. It's a chance you are or not. Regardless, you good. We good." Then he leaned in and kissed my forehead.

SLAM! *The door hit the ground. And for the next sixty seconds my life moved in slow motion.*

Seven fully armed police officers forcefully busted down the door and entered the apartment. They grabbed Snoop and slammed him against the floor. An officer placed his knee in the center of his back and handcuffed him.

"Travis Slaton, you are under the arrest for the murder of Neiman Brown Jr. Anything you say can be used against you in the court of the law. You do have the right to an attorney——"

He was read his rights and then he was escorted out the front door to the cop car. We locked eyes. His facial expression never changed. He didn't say a word. I watched the cops pull off in the storm as the rain pounded against the pavement until the cars vanished in the distance.

Shawn Flossy

ABOUT THE AUTHOR

*Passionate writer. Avid blogger. Former radio host.
Entrepreneur. HBCU graduate.*

Shawn Flossy is a self-published author and founder of PURP Publications. Before venturing into her first novel (The Nightlife Chronicles), Shawn was an avid blogger on her viral erotic fiction blog. As former internet radio host, she sparked debates & entertained listeners for over a year. With more business ventures on the horizon, Shawn releases her sophomore literary piece, *Ally*.

Shawn Flossy

Ally

www.ingramcontent.com/pod-product-compliance
Lightning Source LLC
Chambersburg PA
CBHW050339030726
47503CB00008B/2520